# Timeless Keepsakes

## A Collection of Christmas Stories

Ruth A. Casie
Lita Harris
Emma Kaye
Nicole S. Patrick
Julie Rowe

Timeless Scribes Publishing

Timeless Scribes Publishing LLC

Print ISBN-10: 0991052013
ISBN-13: 978-0-9910520-1-1

Digital ISBN-10: 0991052005
ISBN-13: 978-0-9910520-0-4



Cover created by Alchemy Book Covers and Design
Edited by Mallory Braus
Copy Edited by Michael Mandarano



This edition published by arrangement with Timeless Scribes Publishing LLC.

www.TimelessScribes.com

# Contents

# Introduction
## by Sharon Sala

Holidays mean different things to different people; especially Christmas holidays. Sometimes the memories are all wrapped up in our childhood. Sometimes they become a reminder of what we've lost, rather than rejoicing on where we are. Sometimes we reject them and stay lost in our grief as to how to proceed.

The stories in this most special holiday anthology have a little of something for everyone; stories with vivid reminders of those we've lost; stories where we suspend belief; like a tale told best while under the covers, and being read to us from a book.

There are stories from the present; even a story from an ancient past and the trek to an annual ceremony that ends on a dangerous quest. The telling is often poignant, but with its own brand of happy-ever-after; a kind of 'love you forever' holiday ending that every romantic wants to find at the end of the book.

Whatever the setting, whatever the tale, the common thread among them is the love between a man and woman that leads them to the rest of their life.

Love is timeless, and the keepsakes in each story that trigger the tales are as eclectic as the stories, themselves.

However, when the last page is turned and the last story told, I predict the tales become part of your memory, of one special Christmas and the book you took to your dreams.

Merry Christmas and Happy Holidays,

Sharon Sala
http://www.sharonsala.net

# Mistletoe and Magick

Ruth A. Casie

After a year of searching, Maximilian, the druid Grand Master, finds the sacred mistletoe destined for his soul mate shriveled and dead. He must journey to the Otherworld and tell the Ancestors of his failure.

Ellyn of Brodgar is an exceptional healer. But each healing kiss depletes her energy and brings her closer to death. Ellyn needs to find her own healing power before it's too late.

Max and Ellyn are tossed into the Otherworld and have until the third sunset to appeal to the Ancestors or be lost forever. Together they find love, and as the last rays of the third sunset slip away, both are willing to sacrifice their hopes, dreams, and lives for the other. Do they have what it takes to escape the Otherworld and begin their life together?

Dedicated to ~

My partners and our first self-publishing venture—the first of many! You are all an inspiration and important to me. Thank you for listening to all my crazy ideas and suggestions without laughing.

Paul, whose magick keeps me under his spell.

Mallory Braus, my editor, for her instruction and guidance, and for loving my story as much as I do.

# Mistletoe and Magick
## by Ruth A. Casie

Dead. Maximilian glared at the wilted mistletoe in disbelief. He poked and prodded the plant. It lay there tired and limp. He had cared for the sacred plant for a year. The Ancestors had trusted him to follow their orders. Find a wife—a soul mate. How difficult could it be? All he needed to do was visit the eligible women and choose one. He slammed his fist onto the rough oak table and bellowed his anger to the empty room. Dishes skidded and crashed to the floor. The lifeless shrub didn't move. It didn't change. It sat where he'd put it—robust and healthy—the night before. Now the crumpled brown leaves and withered white berries silently screamed his failure.

He could think of no reason why it hadn't survived. He kept staring at the shriveled plant expecting—no, commanding—it to spring to life. It didn't. He raked his hand through his hair. Everything he'd worked and trained for over the years was lost. He closed his eyes and traveled to that quiet place deep in his mind where he drew his inner strength. One deep breath, then another. His pounding heart took on a more natural rhythm. The reality of his situation hung on his shoulders like an oxen's yoke.

"What's happened? I heard a loud crash." Doward rushed into the cottage and scanned the debris on the floor.

Max didn't trust his voice. He shot the druid councilman a look and pointed to the plant on the table. He registered Doward's unreadable expression and let out a quiet snort. Perhaps that was best. He was grateful his mentor didn't show his disappointment. Doward, too, had warned him.

"One year." Max tipped up his chin and struck a congenial tone. "I'll wager no other Grand Master was forced to relinquish his position after only one year." He turned away, not wanting to see his close friend's disappointment.

"Well," said Doward. "There was Elgon in the year sixty."

Max's head popped up. He hadn't expected Doward to respond. The question had been rhetorical.

"You appear to have forgotten your elementary history lessons." Doward stood shaking an old, crooked finger at him.

Max's mouth opened and closed like a beached fish gasping for air. Only Doward had the nerve, the audacity, to reprimand him. Doward and the Ancestors. He couldn't forget the Ancestors. They had the ultimate power over him.

"Yes, but the Roman invaders killed Elgon at Anglesey." Max's distraction was momentary. He leaned on the table and looked Doward in the eye. "They did not depose him because he couldn't find his soul mate and give her the sacred mistletoe before it died." He straightened, stepped to the cottage door, and stared out at the day but didn't appreciate its sunshine or enjoy the invigorating coolness of the December morning. He turned to Doward. "It simply proves the council made the wrong choice."

"Nonsense." Doward picked up the stray crockery from the floor and set it back on the table. "The council did not make an error. You, my boy," he strode over to Max and clapped him soundly on the back, "were by far the right choice."

"It isn't that I haven't been searching for the woman." He saw the compassion in Doward's eyes. "Surely the Ancestors know I've done that." Even he detected the pleading in his voice and groaned at his weakness.

"Yes, yes." Doward waved his hand as if swatting a fly. "Every eligible woman in the village has gone under your scrutiny."

"Every eligible woman in the village treated me kindly but none were interested in getting close." He rubbed the nape of his neck. "Even when speaking simple pleasantries they avoided looking at me and stepped away." He tried to conceal his frustration but his throat tightened and his voice rose the more he spoke of the women's reactions.

"Perhaps you should have cast a wider net." Doward's tone had turned serious.

Max seethed, having to explain his actions to Doward. "You of all people should know there were more important things that needed to be done."

"But I don't think—"

"Yes, I know," Max interrupted. "You don't think the woman is someone I know or is even amongst the villagers." He glanced at his teacher and softened his voice. "What was I to do? Go from village to village and give every available maiden the mistletoe and see if it thrived?"

"And now? What now?" asked Doward in a gentle tone.

Max turned from the door and sat next to the warm hearth. He rested his elbows on his knees and held his head in his hands as if he sought to overcome a night of too much drink. "I don't know," he whispered. He did know that while he found some of the women beautiful and even enticing, none was his soul mate.

"The ritual of Alban Arthan is tomorrow. You are the Grand Master." Doward stood at Max's shoulder. "It's time for you to travel and meet with the Ancestors in the Otherworld. Only you can carry back their guidance and inspiration for the coming year. And you will have to tell them you haven't found your mate."

"I'm aware," he snapped and regretted his outburst. "Yes," he softened his tone. "I know what I must do." Of course he did. He'd been responsible for the annual ritual for the past five years—four years when he was a high druid and this past year as the Grand Master. Every year was the same. Except last year, they'd presented him with the sacred mistletoe and charged him with finding his soul mate.

"I will go and gather what we need for our journey," offered Doward. "We've delayed as long as we can. I've asked one of the families who set off yesterday to prepare our campsite. But we must leave today."

Max lifted his head and flashed the man a weak smile. "Aye, you go on. I have a few more things to gather. I'll join you shortly."

Doward regarded him thoroughly. After a few seconds he squeezed Max's shoulder. "We will get through this." His mentor took his leave.

He glanced again at the shriveled plant. It had the power to heal everything but itself, it seemed. Doward was right, of course. He would get through this. But would he still be the Grand Master, or reduced to a druid councilman, a priest, or, worse—exiled? He had delayed in order to search his vast library to prepare himself for the consequences and realized he would have the distinction of being the only Grand Master to fail when tasked by the Ancestors. He shuddered inwardly at the idea of failure. It was something he had no practice in.

"Well." He slapped his hands on his knees and rose. He must see this through. He doused the fire, grabbed his half-full pack, and filled it with provisions.

He picked up his warding stones. Perhaps the Ancestors would allow him to train his successor. His chest tightened at the thought. He held the warding stones over the opening of the pouch. But what if the Ancestors had been wrong? He threw the small bundle into his kit and stared at the plant. Somewhere deep inside, a different answer sought light. He turned the problem over in his mind until the solution finally burst through the haze. He smiled at its simplicity and truth. He would go to the Otherworld. Give the Ancestors the withered mistletoe. And tell them he passed their test. There was no soul mate for him.

He carefully wrapped the mistletoe in a clean cloth and put the package into his pouch. Feeling better than he had all morning, he drew on his long wool cloak and closed the cottage door behind him.

"We better hurry along," said Doward, seated on a gelding ready to leave. He searched the sky and rubbed his hands together. "The day grows long and we have a ways to go before we reach Avebury."

Max mounted his horse and together they left the yard. "When you returned from your summer trip to the north, you mentioned the Northern Clan would be joining us this year. I will be glad to see them again."

"Yes, it is always good to see old friends and how their families have grown. The fever struck the clan hard last year. They have suffered many losses. A new healer has settled with them and has been able to help them greatly. When I was there the elder told me he was looking forward to attending this year's ritual. He wants to give thanks to the Great Mother Earth, as he should. He also wants to present the healer to you, for acceptance into his clan."

"Their healer doesn't need my acceptance. Who they choose is up to them."

"Yes, but your acceptance will be an honor for them. It would be good to agree to their request."

"Politics." Max's voice held a hint of disapproval. "I don't have time to play those petty games. Nor do I want people cozying up to me thinking they can influence my decisions."

"You do it quite well. Play politician, that is." Doward rode on quietly.

Max didn't find politics difficult. He had a natural knack for strategy and negotiating. If he admitted it, he thrived on being a leader. But today he wanted to get things done. He didn't want to smile or be nice. No. He wanted to get past this…distraction. He closed his eyes and murmured a short prayer for guidance and for a sign.

The two druid travelers rode up the rise. Before they turned down the wide avenue of oaks Max shifted in his saddle to view his domain—his hearth and home. Satisfied all was in good order, he focused on the trail in front of them and headed northwest toward Avebury.

ഇന്ദ

"Healer," yelled Fendrel, elder of the Northern Clan. The women watched his pacing silhouette from inside their temporary tent. His very pregnant wife, Dimia, peered into the healer's eyes.

"It must be late in the day," said Dimia, lying back on the makeshift pallet.

"Don't fret about the day," said Ellyn as she wrung out the cloth. "It will take care of itself." The healer put the cool cloth on Dimia's forehead. Certain all was well, Ellyn observed the restless shadow on the tent wall. *Will not the man leave us in peace so we can get our work done?*

"How long have we been here? A full day?" The expectant mother ripped off the cloth and flung the rag to the ground. "And still the baby has not birthed." Drenched in sweat, she tried to sit up.

Ellyn stopped her struggle with a touch on the woman's shoulder. The silent signal registered.

"Ellyn, he'll not wait any longer. He's determined to get to the ritual before the ceremony begins. If this baby doesn't come soon the child will simply have to wait until we get to Avebury." Dimia, exhausted more from worrying about her husband than the birth of her first baby, fell back against the pallet.

Ellyn hummed faintly, rinsed out the cloth in the basin filled with melting snow and before she replaced it, tenderly pressed a kiss on the woman's forehead. Already this baby defied his father. She briefly wondered if this was any indication of what the future would bring.

"Healer," Fendrel shouted again.

Ellyn looked from Dimia to the tent flap. Did the man care about his wife? She turned back to her patient whose eyes were half-closed. "Rest easy. I'll be right back."

She put on her cloak and picked up her walking staff. Her hand was ready to push the tent flap aside but she hesitated. "The baby will be a boy," she said over her shoulder. "He will be more like his mother than his father."

A smile spread across Dimia's face. "His father is not so bad." She closed her eyes and took a much-needed rest.

Ellyn stepped out into the forest clearing. The clean, crisp air rushed at her. Snow fell gently and swirled on the puffs of air. Lacy flakes dusted her face. The cool sensation was a welcome relief after the overly warm and cramped sanctuary.

"Finally." Fendrel hurried toward her. "There are only three hours of sunlight left. We have to leave now. We must be there by nightfall." He grabbed her elbow and started to pull her along.

Ellyn yanked her arm away and gave him her best scowl. "Dimia cannot be moved. You could cause great harm to her or the baby, maybe even both, if you moved them now."

A look of indifference colored his face. "One of the other women can bring them along later."

Ellyn raised to her full five feet eight inches and glared at the man. "Fendrel. You are the one who demanded she come to the ritual even though I warned against it. You insisted. Now you will abandon her?" Even she could hear the irritation in her voice.

"Take care, healer. I don't take kindly to your bold speech." He paced in front of her rubbing his chin.

His reprimand did not faze her. She stood silently and waited.

Still pacing, he wagged his finger in the air. "We'll take her with us in the wagon."

"You will not."

Fendrel turned and faced her. "What did you say?"

At the dangerous softening of his voice, she had no doubt she'd gone too far, but she wouldn't let him jeopardize the woman and child.

"You take her to the Alban Arthan ritual in order to show the other clan chiefs your young, fertile bride," she said, determination in her voice. "Arriving with her and your son dead will only suggest you cannot protect them." His eyes widened at the mention of a son. She thought that would get his attention. He had six daughters by his late wife.

She let her words sink in. A quick breeze scurried through the camp. The cold began to creep up her back. She drew her cloak closer.

"Ellyn," cried Dimia.

Ellyn shot Fendrel a look clearly conveying her position was firm.

He dismissed her with a wave of his hand.

Ellyn rushed to the woman, leaving the waiting father where he stood.

Hours later, with the sun sitting low on the horizon, Ellyn came out of the tent and placed Fendrel's new son in his arms.

His eyes were fixed on the baby. "A son." Ellyn didn't miss the reverence in his voice.

"A healthy son and wife. A wife who will bear you more sons," she added for good measure. "What will you name him?"

He gave Ellyn a perplexed look. "We have not thought of a name." His eyes focused on the bundle in his arms and widened with pleasure when the babe yawned. "It will have to be a special name."

"Yes, it will." Perhaps Dimia was right. Fendrel wasn't so bad.

"How is my son's mother?" He strained to peer past the open tent flap into the darkened interior. "After her first outcry I heard nothing."

Ellyn closed the flap. "She bore your son proudly." She wasn't going to tell him the woman bit down on a cloth to keep from screaming. Some things were best not said.

His chest puffed out like a barn rooster. "I knew the minute I caught a glimpse of her she would be a fine breeder."

And here she thought it was Dimia's large breasts and trim waist that'd caught his attention.

"Can I see her? Is she well?" He peered again at the tent.

"She is fine and needs some rest." She didn't miss the man's tender tone. "Let the clan see your son." She started to return to her patient, but hesitated and turned toward him. "You can start getting everyone ready to leave. We won't be long."

His clan gathered round him. "A boy," he said and raised the baby for everyone to see.

Ellyn watched for a moment as Fendrel celebrated his new son. They would have to move swiftly before it got too dark to go on. He needed to get to Avebury. So did she.

ℵ

Max and Doward rode up the ancient earthwork slope that ringed the henge at Avebury and stopped to take in the scene below. The lacy flakes of the soft snow glistened in the waning light and fluttered to the ground. Dusk colored everything in a deepening blue patina. From their vantage point, the pattern of bright yellow campfires that dotted the field easily identified which families had arrived as they took their prescribed place. A flash of a new fire to their left caught their attention.

"Ah, Fendrel has arrived." Doward motioned across the field. "It is good to see their fire burning. Too many years have passed since they last attended."

"I suppose we will have to accept his request and make the ceremony memorable." Max took a sideways glance at Doward. "Right after we greet the winter sun and before I leave for the Ancestors would be a good time."

His mentor shook his head. "That's the most honored portion of the ritual. Sometimes I think you are more a politician than you admit."

Max nudged his horse forward. He led the way down onto the wide causeway and passed the sacred circle. The brisk air was alive with excitement. The familiar tingle of magick ignited him now as it had in the past.

He glanced again at Fendrel's fire. Apprehension skittered across his mind and sent a chill between his shoulders. The rune tattoos on his back warmed. The Ancestors. He would deal with them when the time came. For now he would be the Grand Master the people expected and needed. He let out a deep breath.

He scanned the campfires scattered across the ground and saw the results of his hard work and leadership in uniting the clans and seeing to their well-being. Once again he would stand with them as they gave thanks and honor to the Great Mother Earth.

"I'm looking forward to tonight's campfire," said Doward. "It is good to get reacquainted with old friends, meet their new clan members, and remember those who are gone." They made their way from the causeway. "Ah, there's our campsite." Doward gestured at a gray smudge on a rise beyond where the clans camped.

The men rode through the large camp. By the time they reached their campsite and dismounted, everyone knew the Grand Master had arrived. Max settled their gear while Doward lit the fire.

"Ah, here comes Fendrel," said Doward over his shoulder. "He hasn't wasted any time."

Max cast a glance in time to see the elder making his way up the rise. "It appears he's come by himself." He edged over to the campfire and leaned close to his mentor. "No healer to acknowledge," he whispered.

"Grand Master, how good to see you," shouted Fendrel as he approached.

"I'm glad you decided to join us this year. I hope you had an easy journey. How have you fared?" Max extended an arm and motioned him to take a seat by the fire.

"Many thanks. I am well, as is my clan." The man took the offered seat, which wasn't more than a rug draped over a large stone. "I have much to tell you since I've last been here."

"I understand you have a new wife," said Max. He noted the man's face light up. So, the match was a good one. Somehow that pleased him.

"Not only a new wife but a new son, too." The pride in the man's voice was evident.

Max clapped him on the back. "Congratulations. I would like to meet them both."

"Dimia and my son are with me. They are resting now. You will meet them tomorrow." He paused and gave Max a hesitant look. "I also have a healer who I would like to present to you. She has traveled from Brodgar."

Max glanced at Doward and gave him a knowing smile. "Bring her to me. I will gladly meet her."

Fendrel popped up from his perch. "I will be right back. She wasn't far behind me." Before Max or Doward could say another word he trod over the rise and returned with someone in tow.

Penetrating blue-gray eyes stared out from the cocoon of dark wool that enrobed the woman. The cheeks on her porcelain-white face appeared tinged with a splash of pink. Her natural berry-red lips were turned up in a welcoming smile. "Grand Master." She dipped a well-executed curtsy.

Fendrel's healer was much different than the old crone he had anticipated. This woman was regal and beautiful. The gleam in her eyes was calm and comforting. He had a strange sensation, which made no sense at all, that he had known her for a long time. At ease with her, he allowed himself to relax and returned her open smile with one of his own.

"This is Ellyn of Brodgar," said Fendrel. "She has been our healer for the last year. Our situation was grave. It was her healing skills that kept us alive. I would like you to accept her into our clan."

The knuckles on Ellyn's hand turned white from grasping her staff firmly. Her head whipped around at Fendrel.

Max observed, fascinated the elder was oblivious to the daggers the woman's eyes flung at him. So, Fendrel hadn't told her of his plan and if Max wasn't mistaken, she wasn't pleased.

"Thank you, Fendrel," said Ellyn. "Your request is a great honor. I will be your healer for as long as I am with you." She turned to Max, her face serene. Her iron grip on the staff relaxed.

Fendrel sputtered.

"You are welcome into Fendrel's clan for as long as you see fit to stay with us," said Max. He was certain he saved Fendrel from getting his head bashed with the staff the woman carried. "Brodgar is in the Orkneys. You are far from home."

"I go where I am needed." Her voice was soft—her tone evasive.

Max gave her a benign smile. She was tall and graceful. Loose tendrils of curls softened her face. Dark lashes swept down against her cheekbone. She gazed at him with bright, intelligent eyes. The hairs on the back of his neck stood up. He sensed her trying to press in on his mind and blocked her attempt so fast she winced in pain. He'd made his point. She would not try that again.

"If you will excuse me." She turned to leave. "I would like to look in on Dimia and the baby to make certain they're settled in for the night," she said to the new father.

"Of course, Ellyn. I will see you back to camp." Fendrel approached the two men. "Thank you, Grand Master. Doward. We will see you tomorrow." He and Ellyn went back down the small rise.

"Interesting girl," remarked Doward after they were gone. "You didn't have to be rough on her. She was only curious." Doward chuckled.

Max stared after her.

She wasn't at all what she seemed.

ഇര

"You didn't tell me your stay was temporary." Fendrel stomped across the field toward his tent.

"You didn't ask." Getting angry was useless, so why did she want to bludgeon him with her staff?

"Fendrel," someone shouted from a nearby camp.

"Who's there?" he called, walking toward

the sound. He looked back at Ellyn.

"You go on and visit. I know the way to our campsite," she said.

Fendrel turned back toward the voice. "Gavin? Is that you?" With his hand shading his eyes, he struggled to peer past the bright firelight to see who hailed him.

"Fendrel. You're here," said the tumult of voices.

Ellyn continued without him. The corners of her lips pulled back in a smile. For all his posturing he was a good man. Maybe a bit overenthusiastic. She rubbed her temples, still smarting from the Grand Master's retaliation. Why had she been so bold? When he relaxed and let his guard down the air around him was filled with his distress. It clung to her as if it were her own. Yes, she overstepped her boundary, but he was clearly in pain and something drove her to help him.

A wave of fatigue made her feel as ancient as the Ancestors. Luckily, she could see the campsite in the distance. Eager to rest, she quickened her pace and finally stepped into her tent.

Empty. Dimia must have taken the baby and returned to her husband. Ellyn let out a long, exhausted sigh. She was glad for the solitude and the hot stones left to heat her pallet. That must have been Dimia's work. She smiled and removed her heavy cloak. Dimia was a good match for Fendrel and there would be more children, of that she was certain.

It took a lot of energy to maintain her facade and the Grand Master's reprimand sapped even more of her strength. But she was here, at the ritual. If only she knew why. All year the vision had plagued her. At first it appeared randomly but as the months went by the visions came more often and became more urgent. Now the same scene drifted close to the surface, peeking through at odd times again and again. It was always the same. No more. No less. She stood next to the Grand Master in front of the great oak tree. She had puzzled over it countless times and found no answer.

Perhaps this is how healers end? Called to return their healing gift to the Ancestors in order for it to be passed on to another? For the past year every healing cost her dearly. With each healing kiss she became weaker, her energy drained, and lost more of herself. She knew she was dying. If she were honest, she found the idea of an eternal rest appealing.

She let out a heavy sigh. She gladly helped many but for herself she wanted more, to be part of a clan, a child. Even though people surrounded her, she was alone—her heart was empty. She remembered the tender look on Dimia's face when she first saw her son. She batted away the lone tear that tracked down her cheek.

Well, everything would be clear tomorrow.

Exhausted from the trek, she lay on her pallet and fell asleep before her eyes were closed.

She woke before sunrise refreshed by a good night's sleep. After her morning routine she picked up her staff and joined the others at the standing stones. Today, the shortest day of the year, they would welcome the day and celebrate the sacred marriage between Father Sky and Mother Earth. She waited while Doward finished cleansing and purifying the area for the Grand Master.

Ellyn and the people from all the clans proceeded through the outer circle to the Cove and its three standing stones. Doward came up to her. "Another year. They seem to hurry by."

A wave of unease washed over her. She hardly made out what Doward said. She was too busy trying to control her rising apprehension.

The clans formed a large circle around the stones and waited. The Grand Master walked down the wide avenue and took his place. He stood beside her. She had imagined his tall, commanding presence quite correctly.

Everyone in the large circle faced east and waited for the sun to peek over the horizon. Slowly sunlight crept up and bathed the central Cove stone with its first rays of light.

"Hail and welcome," declared Max.

"Hail and welcome," the clans around him responded.

In unison they faced the center of the large circle.

"Hail this new day and year. We remember those who have left us. And we welcome those who have joined us by marriage, birth, or simply by choice." He nodded toward Ellyn. "Ellyn of Brodgar, we welcome you into Fendrel's clan."

"Thank you, Grand Master." Ellyn's voice carried loud and clear. She faced Fendrel. "Thank you for making a place for me at your hearth."

The first part of the morning ritual completed, the circle broke. She followed Max and the others as they made their way to the great oak in the nearby grove.

"Are you familiar with this part of the ritual?" asked Doward.

"Yes. The Grand Master will enter the Otherworld and meet with the Ancestors."

"There is more to the ritual," said Doward. "To ensure a good year and banish evil, when the Grand Master returns with the message from the Ancestors, the women will cut down and collect springs of mistletoe from the sacred oak tree. The Grand Master will give the sprigs to the families in the clan for them to hang in their house."

Everyone gathered around the ancient oak. Once again she and Doward stood in the great circle next to the Grand Master.

Max waited for quiet before he faced the east and raised his arms. "Hail, Guardians of the East. I summon the power of air." His voice echoed through the grove.

"By the air in her breath, be with us now," the congregation replied.

He turned to the south. "Hail, Guardians of the South. I summon the power of fire."

"By the fire in her spirit, be with us now," came the reply.

He faced the west. "Hail, Guardians of the West. I summon the power of water."

"By the waters of her womb, be with us now."

Turning north he said, "Hail, Guardians of the North. I summon the power of earth."

"By the earth that is her body, be with us now." Every eye turned to Max when he faced the ancient oak, mistletoe hanging in great bunches from its mighty branches.

"As above, so below.
As within, so without.
Four stars in this place be

To open the door to the Ancestors to me."

The cold air chilled even more and the sky turned an array of colors. Every muscle in Ellyn's body tensed. This was magick she was not supposed to see. She must be too close to the Grand Master. She struggled to move away but was fixed to the spot. Slowly the world began to spin. She took a few deep breaths to steady herself, planted her staff deep into the ground, and held on. She peered through a hazy filter and witnessed Doward's nod. She studied his lips silently mouthing, *Safe journey.*

The cold wind pricked her skin like hundreds of tiny needles. She closed her eyes and firmly held on to her staff.

Shiver after shiver made her shoulders quake. She had never been so cold. A strong hand covered hers. She strained to pull away but it held her fast. The muffled chant in a deep baritone voice washed over her. The cold shivers melted into a comforting warmth and the tempest calmed.

When she opened her eyes the swirling had stopped. The weather was agreeable but the Grand Master's expression was deadly.

"What are you doing in the Otherworld? How did you get here?" He pulled his hand away from hers.

She removed her staff from the ground. "I have no idea. I stood by you during the ritual but many others did too."

"The portal only obeys the command of the Ancestors. My powers are limited here. I have no way to send you back." He ran his hand through his hair and paced in front of her.

Standing tall, she waited and spoke not a word. Curious, she looked around.

The Otherworld. This was a place of stories, not reality. The dark silhouettes of the trees and bushes were dramatic against the deep blue of the retreating night. The sweeping clouds brightened with vivid colors of magenta and red. The waking sounds of the forest were soft and clear. The oak they stood near took her breath away. The light caught the morning dew on its bare branches and made them twinkle like thousands of sparkling gems.

She didn't look at the Grand Master. She was certain there would be murder in his eyes.

ꕥ

"I can't leave you here." He cleared his throat. "You'll have to come with me," he droned on.

"You can leave me here." She spun around and followed the flight of two butterflies that caught her attention as they fluttered by.

"No, I can't." He ground the words out between clenched teeth. "Don't let the tranquil beauty fool you," he said with quiet emphasis, trying to contain his anxiety. "It's difficult traveling in the Otherworld alone. This place is not like any other. The Otherworld has traps and villains. They are just well hidden." A muscle flicked angrily at his jaw.

"Yes, Grand Master. I will keep your warning in mind." She waited, her hands folded in front of her.

"We may be here for a while." His eyes searched the horizon.

"A while?" Her brows furrowed. "You must be back by the full rise of the moon."

He gave her a stare with hard gray eyes that were like silver lightning. “Time is different in the Otherworld. We must meet the Ancestors within three days. They will return us to the oak at moonrise. To everyone there we will return the evening we departed.”

Her eyes widened and her brows arched in surprise. “How curious.”

He nodded toward the forest. “We’re going there. Follow me closely. We’re searching for a rope bridge. It should be nearby.”

They crossed a small clearing. Max held up his hand and brought them to a stop. “Wait here.” He started off.

“Is anything wrong?” she asked.

“I’m not certain.” He hesitated and searched her face, debating whether to tell her he had no idea where they were. Usually he arrived standing at the rope bridge. Today was different.

“I want to see what is behind that thicket. Wait here.” He moved off the path and headed toward the undergrowth.

Murmured voices rode on the breeze. She couldn’t make out what they said but as the breeze buffeted around her, they became more insistent. Trying to stay calm, she stared where the Grand Master had vanished. A vision of him in danger slammed behind her eyes. She took off at a run. She made her way to the other side of the thicket and skidded to a stop in front of a broken bridge platform. A wide gorge loomed in front of her. On the other side she made out a matching platform with the walkway dangling from its supports. She tenuously moved to the rim of the cliff and glanced to either side. There was no one there. She peered over the edge and was filled with relief. Within arm's reach, the Grand Master climbed up what remained of the rope bridge, a small rock outcropping below him.

"Grand Master," she called.

"Aye," he said as his head popped over the edge. She gave him her hand.

He stared at her outstretched hand in disbelief. "You can't pull me up." He panted and strained to find a hold. "We'll both go down."

When he found none, his eyes widened and he began to slide backward. Ellyn grabbed his arm and tugged. Putting her full weight behind it, she dragged him up far enough for his other hand to find a hold. He scrambled over the top and lay face down panting at her feet. His tunic was bloody and in shreds. She examined the deep scrapes clawed into his back by the face of the cliff. It would take time for these wounds to heal. Time they didn't have.

"I thought they called out and I followed," said Max.

"Who called out?" she asked.

"The Ancestors, of course. This is the shortest way to the standing stones. I was too eager. I knew something was amiss." He winced in pain. "I should have listened to my own words," he said between clenched teeth.

"Yes. There are traps and villains everywhere," she mimicked his words. She opened the pouch she wore at her waist and removed a vial. "You must have slid down on your back. The scrapes are deep." Before she took care of his wounds she pressed her lips tenderly on his head, a kiss she was certain he would not feel. But his muscles twitched in response. She gasped in surprise at his reaction.

"I stepped onto the platform. It was fine." He yawned. "But when I moved to the walkway the ropes gave way and I was falling through the air…" His voice trailed off and his eyelids slid closed.

She tenderly touched the rune tattoos on his back and gaped as each touch made them glow. She heard the tales of the magick runes but thought they were just that, tales. She stared at him, unable to say a word. She worked quickly, checking every scrape. His wounds dressed and bandaged, she massaged his shoulders. When she was satisfied his muscles were relaxed, she gently prodded him to roll onto his back. The scrapes on his chest told a different story. These appeared to be minor.

Kneeling beside him, she ministered those scrapes as well. When she was done, she sat back on her heels, startled. "Well, Grand Master, that is as much as I can do. The rest is up to you."

"Aye," he said sleepily, followed by a soft snore.

She wiped the blood from the scratches on his cheek and studied him.

Full brows framed his wide-set eyes with long, thick lashes. His high cheekbones accentuated the deep hollows beneath them. His close-clipped beard outlined his full lips. His face spoke of power and ageless strength. He had a face that was easy to look at.

The wounds cleaned and bandaged, she bent over and gave him a lingering kiss on his forehead. Her head snapped up and her fingers went to her lips. They tingled as if she had eaten something spicy. She searched his face. His ashen color hadn't changed. Panic welled in her throat. Her healing kiss always brought results.

His arm snaked around her and drew her to him. She didn't resist when he drew her closer and kissed her deeply. When she moved away his eyes were closed, the corners of his mouth tipped up in a smile, and his face took on a soft pink hue.

Relief flooded through her but was quickly replaced with doubt. For the first time she wondered if her healing kiss would be enough.

She prepared the camp and when she was done, sat back to rest. The smell of the wood and the snap of the fire were soothing. The dancing flames mesmerized her and drew her in deeper. The intertwined flames parted and in its midst she saw two figures following a light. She knew it was an omen but she could not tell if the sign was good or bad. A loud snap and a log fell, sending sparks flying, startling her out of her trance.

Drained. She anticipated the numbing feeling before it overcame her. She made herself as comfortable as possible—some tea and honey would renew her. Perhaps this was why she needed to be here. To make certain the Grand Master completed the ritual and returned. Still confused as to why she was with him, there was nothing to do but wait and see.

"You're awake."

He scanned the camp and found her sitting nearby licking her fingers. Bolts of heat pulsed through him as his eyes followed her tongue stroking each digit. He pulled his gaze from her tantalizing tongue to her face. He was greeted by her warm and genuine smile.

"I thought you would sleep until spring." She stepped over to the fire and poured another cup.

"How long have I slept?" He glanced at the sun and judged it was midmorning.

"If the sunrise and set is to be believed, one day. How do you feel?"

Resting on the stone-strewn ground wrapped in his cloak, he stretched to work out the kinks that settled in his back. Blinking his eyes, everything came into focus. Did she say one day? He pulled himself up on his elbows.

She rushed and put a hand on his chest. "Not so quickly. Get up slowly."

He sat up and took the offered hot drink.

"I found some supplies amongst your things. It's fortunate you carried them with you."

One whiff told him the liquid was laced with honey. He chuckled. "The first time I came to the Otherworld I took no provisions. Three days without food was…difficult." He observed her over the rim of the cup. Her sluggish movements and drawn face told him she hadn't slept well.

"I didn't pack any honey," he said, looking into the cup.

"No. I found a nearby hive and the bees were more than willing to share."

"One day spent," he said, more to himself. "We must go. We have to—"

"—be back at Avebury by tomorrow's moonrise. I know." She handed him something to break the fast.

He took the oatcake from her and ate hungrily. "What have you done all this time?"

"Admired the view." She nodded at where he slept.

He followed her gaze. He lay in the middle of a pentagram with glistening gems set correctly at each point. He searched the area looking from side to side, panic spread across his face.

"Is this what you're seeking?" She held out his pouch.

"Yes." Relief rushed through him. He rummaged inside the leather bag. "Everything will be for naught if it's gone," he said.

"For naught?"

"I have to give the Ancestors this sacred mistletoe." He held up the wrapped cloth. Hoping for a miracle, he held his breath and peeked inside. But the air rushed out of him when he saw the plant's brown leaves. Disappointed and resigned, he replaced the package into his pouch and set it down. As he did, his eyes caught the gleam of the warding stones.

"What worried you that you set the wards?" His voice rang with concern. He had sensed no threat. Surely if he had he would have found the strength to set the wards. A cold sweat dampened his brow. Were his powers weakening? Would the Ancestors take action without hearing him out?

"A…feeling. That was all. I've learned to trust them. Besides, you were…vulnerable while you slept," she spoke plainly.

"You have set wards and protected the area well for a healer." He finished the last of the sparse meal. "A spae-woman?" He saw her with a new measure of respect.

"And what do you know of spae-women?" Her quiet voice held some measure of a challenge.

"They are skilled healers and are known for their ability to see events before they happen. On your island they are treated with a holy respect." His tone was matter-of-fact. "I value the old ways and those trained in them." He ran his hand down the healed marks on his chest. That explained why his wounds healed so fast. He flexed his back muscles while he shrugged into his clean tunic. "Many thanks for tending to me. You are indeed a special person." He focused on her lips. The thought of them tender and swollen took him by surprise. The runes on his back warmed. A warning? No, the Ancestors called. He rose in one fluid motion onto somewhat unsteady feet. "And for keeping us both safe. We should move on as soon as possible."

ꙮ

"We have to cross the gorge." He stood on the wooden platform that anchored the bridge, fished up the rope guidelines that had supported the walkway, and inspected them.

Ellyn peered over his shoulder. "The rope isn't worn." She pointed to the end in his hand. "It's been cut."

Max threw the rope over the side. His surprise turned into white-hot anger. Were the Ancestors so displeased with him that they would put his life in jeopardy? Was Ellyn their target? He studied the healer. Her face was full of strength, shining and steadfast. Based on her reaction in the portal she knew nothing of the Otherworld. If he hadn't held her in place who knew where she would have been taken. No, she was here by accident.

He was fortunate. If anything happened to him she could go back to Avebury to deliver the message to the people. Accident or destiny? His anger faded into misery as understanding flashed through him—what if they would not let him return? His final test must be to get her safely to the Ancestors. So be it. He picked up the warding stones and dragged his foot through the pentagram while murmuring a silent prayer for guidance. Ellyn put together the rest of their meager belongings. He glanced up and down the gorge. "There." He pointed to the right. "The other way across."

"A land bridge?" asked Ellyn.

"Yes, that is the only other way across."

"I'm ready if you are." She stood by the trail with her staff in hand.

Max shouldered his pouch, led them back through the thicket, and down the trail.

"I gather this isn't usually what happens," she said.

"No." He hesitated. "They called me to the thicket. I knew I had to go alone."

"Is this place inhabited by anyone else? I mean, anyone other than the Ancestors? I always imagined they were the only ones in the Otherworld. I thought the voices were theirs."

He shortened his pace to match hers. "Voices?"

"Yes. After you went through the thicket I heard something. I couldn't make out what they said. They were hushed and rode on the gusts of wind but as I waited the wind got stronger and the voices more intense. Are you certain no one else is here?"

"Only the Ancestors. If the rope was cut, they must have cut it." The idea of an outright attack still mystified him. He hadn't heard any warning. On the contrary, they lured him to the cliff and all but pushed him over. Misery tore at his insides at the thought they had abandoned him.

"The rock ledge appears to be all that prevented you from falling to the bottom of the gorge," said Ellyn.

If it hadn't been for that ledge…well, he didn't want to think what would have happened. What he did think about was fighting for what he wanted—not just to live another day but to continue to lead his people. He trudged on with Ellyn, determined to make his case before the Ancestors.

After several hours, they arrived at the edge of the forest. "We'll stop here for a while."

She looked up at the sun to get her bearings. "It's not quite midday."

"Yes, but the rest of the way is a steep downhill climb. We won't be able to move as fast."

"It's just as well we stop. I want to remove the bandages and make certain the wounds have not putrefied. You'll need to take off your tunic." She took out the vials and bandages from her pouch.

Max stood two arm-lengths in front of her and removed his garment.

She couldn't look away from him. His appearance was deceptive. He wasn't a warrior's size—she had tended many of them with their broad, barrel-like chests. This man was tall and trim. His torso appeared defined, lean, and sinewy. His muscled arms looked powerful and she craved to have them around her. They could keep her safe forever. Her desire for his touch was painfully deep. She forced herself to turn away. This was not like her. Was it this place? Did it strip her bare of all pretense to show her who she really was? Was this the reason for being here?

"Your wounds appear well healed." She stared into his eyes and something sensuous passed between them.

"Perhaps you should take a closer look. To make certain." His voice sounded like velvet.

His soft voice teased her. They played a dangerous game, one she should not play. She imagined his arms around her, his lips on hers, and heat flashed through her. Dazed by the depth of the sensation, her resolved began to falter. Perhaps just a little pleasure, something to remember. After all, he would return to Avebury soon.

She closed the gap between them and ran her hand over his healed scars. Each gentle touch made her fingers tingle. She did not pull her hand away. The air around them was charged and alive. She laid her palm on his chest and flinched at his quick intake of breath. So, he sensed it too.

"The scratches are healed. You can hardly see where they were." Her voice was a whisper.

"Yes, I know." He brushed her long hair away from her face and held her head in the cup of his hand. "You are an extraordinary healer."

Reluctantly, she stepped away and broke the spell they had cast. *Coward,* she said to herself. *Keeping your heart safe will not save you from your destiny.* With shaking hands she put the vials back into her pouch and picked up her staff.

"Here, you can put this back on." She handed him his tunic but it appeared his attention was elsewhere. The garment fell to the ground, forgotten. She followed his gaze as he looked around them.

"Max?"

He raised his fingers to his lips. She got his silent signal—quiet.

A rumbling in the woods caught Ellyn's attention. Instinct took over—she focused on one direction and opened her mind. The breeze stopped. The soft sounds around them went silent. *There!* She turned to Max and attempted to move but she couldn't. Panic consumed her. She tried again but she was chained to the spot. *There!* She fought to call to him but no sound came out of her mouth. The Grand Master, his back to her, concentrated on the wrong direction. Determined, she jabbed her staff to the ground in protest and demanded the elements answer her. Obedience was immediate. The barrier that held her shattered in a shower of fine crystal. She raced forward and reached him in time to shove him out of the path of an attacking boar.

The boar turned for another attack. They both grabbed her staff. In a burst of light, the startled boar stood still. She let go and gave Max the staff. The boar faced them pawing the ground. It shook its head, the foot-long, curved-bone tusks glistening in the light.

Max sidestepped to the right to get some distance between himself and Ellyn. The boar swiveled its head from Max to Ellyn as if trying to make up its mind who to attack. The boar sniffed the air and approached Ellyn.

Ellyn didn't move. She kept her eyes on the animal and worked hard to stay calm. Max stamped the staff on the ground and bellowed his war cry. The boar stopped. Its muscles quivering with tension, it turned and charged at Max, forcing him toward the large boulders by the cliff.

The crack of her staff and the squeals and grunts from the boar went on as Max successfully kept the boar at bay. Little by little, Max moved the boar farther away from Ellyn and closer to the cliff.

Facing each other, the boar pawed the ground and bellowed in frustration. Finally, it charged at Max.

Max stood still and waited. The boar came closer. The ground rumbled as the animal gained speed. Max held his position. When the beast was an arm's length from Max he stepped to the side. The animal flew at him and careened over the cliff.

Ellyn ran to Max. They stood and gaped as the animal tumbled through the air and dissolved into nothing. It never hit the ground.

She stared in disbelief at the empty space where the animal plunged. She looked back at the Grand Master. His bruised and bloodied body indicated a different story. She didn't ask questions. It appeared the Otherworld had its own rules.

"Sit here." She once again prepared to help him.

"The scrapes are nothing." He sat on a rock as she requested. "The animal wasn't real." He pointed out to the gorge.

"The animal may not have been real but your bruises and scrapes are. I didn't see the animal strike you. I don't know how you got these wounds."

"The Ancestors are playing with us," he muttered.

Ellyn leveled her gaze and gave him a serious look.

"Perhaps they want you to give me another healing kiss?" His smile was mischievous. "I may ask them for more challenges."

Her hand trembled when she reached out to swab the wounds. He grabbed it. "I was only making jest. To break the tension. I meant no disrespect."

"I know. We are both tired." She kept at her work.

"Your staff…"

"Yes, what about my staff?" She continued to dab at the scrapes on his chest.

"It glowed when we both held it."

She stopped her ministrations, her hand in midair. "It's only glowed once before. When I first touched it. My father believed it recognized me." She kept working her way across his chest and down his forearm. "The staff is ancient. Its secret has been lost over time. I thought it only glowed for its owner. Perhaps it wants to belong to you."

She traced her finger over each wound. Every touch warmed her in the most personal places, followed by delightful shivers of desire. She tamped down her feelings. The Ancestors had a sense of humor. How could she find someone now when she was dying? He was a bit crusty on the outside but she knew there was a softer, kinder side to him. Somehow her destiny was caught up in his. *Are the Ancestors testing my healing to see if it is worthy? Perhaps they need proof that it is strong before they take it back and give it to another. I won't let them have it until Max is safe.*

If it was the last thing she did, she would protect him. He had to carry the message back. The people depended on him.

She cleaned the last wound. Gently she caressed his head in her hands and placed a healing kiss on his forehead. "For the Ancestors."

Max slowly stood. Tenderly he tilted up her chin and kissed her forehead. "For the Ancestors."

His breath bathed her cheek and she closed her eyes.

He kissed each eye before he planted a searing kiss on her lips. He took her in his arms. "This attack was too close. You're in too much danger."

"It was you who was bruised and scraped."

She rested her head on his chest and enjoyed his strong, steady heartbeat.

He tormented her with his kisses, built a heat in her that was both frightening and delightful. She wanted him to touch her in the most inappropriate places and from his actions believed he did too. But she couldn't entertain those feelings. How could she encourage him when she knew he had no future with her? No, she had to keep him away. The thought stabbed her deeply but she knew she was right. Time with him was too short but it would have to last her a lifetime. Her energy seeped away more each day. If she didn't get to the Ancestors soon she feared there would be nothing remaining of her for them to see.

Max put his arm around her waist. "The Ancestors are not much farther."

They moved on and arrived at the land bridge at sunset.

"There are many pitfalls hidden there." He ran his hand through his hair. "We'll have to wait until morning." He searched the perimeter where they stood. The area appeared safe and as good a spot to rest for the night as any other. She worked at his side but one look at her drawn and weary face told him she couldn't have gone on much further.

She stared at the land bridge. "Something is not right." She paced back and forth like a caged animal.

"What bothers you?"

"How long will it take us to cross the bridge?"

"A day." The humor was gone from his voice.

"We only have one more day. If we face any delays on the other side we will be out of time. What happens if we don't find the Ancestors in three days?" He heard the determination in her voice.

He approached and studied her closely. "You know, don't you? You see events before they happen." He grabbed her by the shoulders and almost shook the answer from her. "What did you see?"

"Max, let me go," she said.

Stunned by her thin, weak voice and shocked by his own actions, his eyelids slid closed and he clutched her to his chest. "What did you see?" he asked her tenderly.

"I see us following a light but I cannot tell you what it is, where it leads, or if it is a good or bad omen. That's what scares me most." She hesitated. "I'm…tired. I have no energy to coax a deeper vision."

"Rest. We'll cross the bridge tomorrow. We will find the Ancestors and go home to Avebury."

Ellyn woke in the morning and found a gray mist covering the ground. The campfire was out and Max was gone. She shot up, wrapped herself in her cloak, and picked up her staff.

"Where are you going?"

She turned toward his voice. Max entered the camp, a load of wood in his arms.

"I was going to search for you."

He dropped the wood by the fire pit.

"When do you want to leave?" she asked.

He pointed to the gray wall of fog. "We're not going anywhere. We'll have to wait until the fog lifts."

"You have no idea how long that will be. It could be days."

"Or it could be hours. Ellyn, if we did get across the bridge I won't be able to see any of the landmarks to lead us to the Ancestors. We will have to stay where we are until the fog clears."

He lit the fire and she sat close to it to keep out the dampness. When her legs stiffened, she paced the small area until she knew the number of steps in every direction. Tired of tramping around and getting nowhere, she returned to the fire. The ritual repeated over and over, making each passing hour tedious. Finally, Ellyn leaped up. "I can't wait any longer."

Startled, Max appeared at her side. "What are you doing?"

She wrapped her cloak around her closely and got her staff. "I'm going to find the Ancestors. You can stay if you like but I'll not let this day end without finding them."

"We can't go out there. I don't know if I can keep you safe."

She searched his face. “Is that why we have stayed in this place? To keep me safe?” Her heart skipped a beat at the confirmation that he cared. “Thank you, Max, but staying here won’t solve our problem. We need to get to the Ancestors before the end of the day. You need to give them the mistletoe. And they need to send you back to Avebury.” She rested her hand on his arm. “We need to move now.”

“Yes, you’re right. I can’t stop what is fated.” He let out a deep breath.

She gave him a questioning stare but did not pursue the issue. They doused the fire, took their belongings, and picked their way across the narrow walkway.

“It must be midafternoon.” Max checked the outline of the sun through the thick clouds. He stood at the beginning of the steep decline. “We haven’t much farther to go. This is the deep fissure we have to manage through. We’ll have to climb down and up the other side.”

She nodded her understanding.

The first part of the descent wasn’t too difficult. As they continued on, loosened rocks tumbled down in front of them. In some areas Max slid as if he skated on ice. He helped her down, blocked her slide, and made the climb as easy for her as he could. Finally at the bottom of the fissure, they both scanned the steep climb ahead of them.

“I’ve only been this way once.” He moved back from the cliff wall trying to see through the mist. “I think I see the sun. I want to look at what we face.” He turned to Ellyn. “I’ll go up a bit, see how thick the mist is, and look for an easy way up.”

Her face blanched. “Perhaps we should

make the climb together," she said. "If anything happens, the other would be near."

He took off his pouch, still evaluating the cliff. "That won't be necessary. I promise not to get into any trouble without you," he said with a smile. "I'll leave these with you. Take care of the mistletoe. I will be back with good news." He got a good handhold and scaled up the face of the cliff.

As he moved up he sent a shower of small stones raining down. At least she knew he was moving on the wall.

"The mist seems to be thinning," he shouted down to her.

"Can you see the top?" she called.

"No, but I am walking rather than crawling up the side."

She sank to the ground and waited.

"Max," she called.

He didn't answer.

"Max," she shouted urgently. She knew she should have insisted on going with him. In a panic she sprang up and spilled the contents of his pouch on the ground. She searched for handholds in the stone to climb up after him.

"Ellyn, can you hear me? The fog is clearing. I see an easy way for us to get up the cliff. I'm coming down."

"Yes, I hear you." Relieved, she sank to the ground and waited. Her hand found the spilled contents of Max's pouch. She picked up each item and put it back. When she picked up the rolled cloth it came undone. The sacred mistletoe lay on the ground shriveled and dead. She stared at the withered plant then up at the cliff. He had to take the mistletoe to the Ancestors. He couldn't give them a dead plant. She raised the plant to her lips and kissed it. For Max.

The shriveled brown leaves unfolded in her palm. The edges sparkled as if they were on fire. The glow traced the fragile veins of the leaves until she held a glowing lace network. New life surged through the plant as the glow faded and turned a healthy green. Next the withered berries pulsed and plumped until they were filled out and white. She rolled the renewed mistletoe into the cloth and replaced it in Max's pouch.

"If the fog hadn't lifted I would never have found this path." He stepped out from around a boulder not far from her. "It's an easy trail." He stopped midstep when he saw her. "Ellyn." He ran to her. Her eyes were dark hollows and her face was ashen. She rocked back and forth, clutching his pouch. Fear like he'd never known before welled in his chest. He had to get her to the Ancestors. They would know what to do.

He lifted her into his arms and with long, determined strides navigated up the twisted path. The higher they got, the brighter the sunlight.

"When we are back in Avebury we will celebrate our journey."

She laid her head against his chest.

Worried by her shallow breathing, he pushed himself and quickened his pace. He glanced at her face. Were her eyes brighter? He hoped he was right. "You're not going to speak to me?"

She tipped her face toward him and smiled at his admonishment. "What do you want me to say?" she asked so quietly he almost didn't hear her.

"Tell me the secret of your healing."

"You know I can't tell you."

"I thought at first it was magick in the vials you keep, but I think your magick is more potent than a potion." He stepped onto the top of the cliff and into a pool of warm sunlight. He turned and they both glanced back over the route they'd taken. The sun sat low, near the horizon but not yet set.

"There is still time," he told her. The smell of the wild forest, the feel of the cooling breeze across his back, and even the taste of wild herbs on the air, sharpened his senses as he pressed on. He was getting closer. He stepped into a large clearing.

"Ellyn. The standing stones. And it's not yet sunset." His voice was alive with excitement.

"Max, leave me there and go speak to the Ancestors." She pointed to the pool of sunlight.

He hesitated, not wanting to leave her. "Are you certain? I don't want to be far from you."

"I'll be right here. You must speak to them alone."

She was right. Gently he put her down inside the outer circle of stones on a soft patch of grass and covered her with his cloak. "Rest here. I shouldn't be long." He started off.

"Max." She kissed the pouch before she handed it to him. "For good luck."

He bent down and kissed her tenderly.

"You needn't worry." She settled herself and smiled at him. "Now go. We've taken long enough."

He quickly navigated toward the sacred inner circle and glanced up as the blood red hunter moon began its climb. A cold knot formed in his stomach. The blood moon was not a good omen.

ஐ

Max approached the inner stones with more confidence than he felt.

"As above, so below.

As within, so without.

The Grand Master and Healer in this place be,

Ask the Ancestors to speak to me."

A swirl of clouds filled the center space.

He stood by the stone altar. The mist thickened in deep pools and drifted to the bottom of the great sarsen stones. Churning like a phantom stew, fingers of mist crept up the stones, leaving a shimmering outline in its wake. The silhouette thickened, revealing the hooded forms of the Ancestors.

"Grand Master, who do you bring to the sacred circle?"

"The healer—" his voice boomed.

"Only you, the Grand Master, are permitted to approach us for our guidance." The angry voice of an Ancestor reached his ears. "But we are forgiving."

"I come to seek—"

"Before you tell us what you seek, tell us of your quest."

A flicker of apprehension pulsed through him. He was certain Ellyn didn't have much time and the full red moon hung large in the sky. Only a thin arc of sun remained on the horizon.

He removed the wrapped cloth from his pouch and laid the package on the altar stone. "I have passed your test." He did not expose the mistletoe. He didn't want the Ancestors to see the dead plant, not until he had Ellyn safely back to Avebury. After that he didn't care.

"You have found your mate?"

Max hesitated. "Perhaps. I have much to tell you, but before I begin I ask for a boon." He glanced over his shoulder. She waited for him.

"What do you seek?" the Ancestors rumbled with a cold, hard voice.

"Ellyn of Brodgar is ill. I ask you to help her. She is honorable and has served the people well and denies no one at her own expense."

"You are the people's Grand Master. She is your responsibility. We can only guide and help those who have passed on to our world."

"No," he insisted, pounding his fist on the stone altar. How could this be? For the first time in his life he felt helpless. He could not lose her. He knew if he did he would lose a part of himself. "She has done everything—"

"It is not for us to interfere." The voice was calm and without empathy.

"You do not interfere? You demanded I find a mate."

There was no response.

He tried to keep his control. "She told me she was compelled to come here. Why?"

Still they did not respond.

Anger surged through him. "You brought her here. She needs your help. She's dying." He pointed to where he left her.

"Only you can help her, Grand Master."

"Me?" He stopped short. "How? If I could she'd already be cured."

"Why do you care what happens to her? She is just a simple Orkney witch. Nothing else."

Ideas flashed across Max's mind. If he was the only one that could help her the answer must lie in his greatest gift. His magick. He must get her back to Avebury, back to his magick, before the sun set.

"Here." He unrolled the mistletoe. "Here is your talisman. Send us back to Avebury," he demanded.

"So, you found your mate," said the Ancestor with a satisfied voice.

Max looked at the healthy mistletoe and gaped in astonishment. The plant was dead when he'd last looked. How could it now be alive? Icy fear raced up his back. He glanced at Ellyn on the far side of the circle. Her kisses. All this time he teased her and it was her kiss all along.

"You hold her destiny in your hands."

His eyes moved from the mistletoe to the Ancestors.

"I don't understand." He gave the Ancestors a questioning stare.

"It appears that with her last breath she has made certain you will succeed. Is there any other way for her to prove herself to you?" voiced one Ancestor.

"No," Max whispered. "Not her last breath."

"No? Were you not willing to fight, sacrifice yourself, to save her?" said another Ancestor. "Can you not see the love in your heart for her?"

"Then why these tests?" he demanded. "Am I not worthy? Is she not worthy?" he asked, spacing the words out evenly.

"This was not your test," said the Ancestor.

Not a test? "Then what?" Anger rolled off him in waves. "The time we've wasted, the pain she's suffered." He fisted his hand and forced himself to remain calm. "What would have happened if we didn't find each other?" he demanded.

"It is fortunate for you both that you did," said the Ancestor.

Max lowered his head and stared at the ground. His mind raced to think of a way to save Ellyn.

"You both needed to find your soul mates. We provided opportunities. For both of you. But know that, in time, your love for each other will be greatly tested. Your love will have to be very strong for that…test."

Max raised his head. Of course their love was strong. His eyes found the altar. The mistletoe, alive and healthy, caught his attention. A ray of hope blossomed. Max grabbed the mistletoe from the altar. "We will be ready for your tests when the time comes."

He rushed to Ellyn and held the mistletoe under her nose. Silently he begged her to breathe deeply but he saw no response; instead she shivered.

He knew from her shallow breaths and pale skin that she didn't have much longer.

"Don't leave me, Ellyn. Not when I've just found you," he demanded. Distraught, he could think of nothing else but to hold her and love her.

He rested the mistletoe on the rock ledge above her head. "Stay with me," he murmured in her ear. Her eyes closed, he kissed them, and moved on to her lips. With her cradled in his arms, he held her to his heart, and silently prayed. He witnessed the sun slip below the horizon and the last remnants of light darken—their fate sealed.

Her eyes fluttered open and a smile spread across her face. “I dreamt of you, Grand Master,” she said in a sleepy voice.

He looked deeply into her eyes and held her close. “My heart,” he murmured in her ear. “Oh, is it Grand Master now? I much prefer Max.” He let the realization of his love for her wash over him. “Ellyn. I have much to tell you.” He spoke with as reasonable a voice as he could manage.

She put her fingers to his lips.

He searched her face. Yes, her eyes were brighter and the dark hollows surrounding them were almost gone. He brushed her cheek with his fingertips. She was warm and in the fading light he thought her ashen pallor was fading. Max glanced at the mistletoe.

“I know, Max.” She peered deeply into his eyes. “I know what is to come.”

He held her tight. “I almost lost you,” he whispered.

“I love you. You are my greatest gift,” she declared.

He broke away for a moment. “And you, mine. I love you, Ellyn.” He bent down to kiss her again but she held him off. She turned her face to the moon.

“The sun is gone and moonrise is almost complete. We’re too late,” she spoke in a weak, trembling whisper.

He grabbed the mistletoe and gave it to her. “Hold this.” He scooped her up and hurried back to the inner circle.

“Max, don’t do this. It is forbidden.”

“I’ve been a fool. I would give anything for

you to be well. Anything for us to be together." He came into the inner circle.

"You are fortunate, Grand Master," said the Ancestor.

Max halted and gave the Ancestor a questioning stare. He stood with Ellyn next to him.

"You must return to the great oak before the full moonrise," said the Ancestor, motioning to the moon.

Max turned and watched the great shadow cover the orb. "Thank you. I am humbled." He bowed his head.

"You have the sacred mistletoe." The Ancestor pointed to the sprig Ellyn held. "Guard it well. But know that the mistletoe did not heal you. Only the love of your soul mate could do that."

"Yes, I know." Ellyn stood at Max's side. She planted her great staff solidly in the ground between them. Max's hand covered hers on the staff—it glowed.

"Your mighty staff knows the truth. Its light will always lead you to each other, amongst other things, but—" said the Ancestor.

She and Max looked first at her staff then at the Ancestors.

"I have foreseen the future and I go willingly," said Ellyn. "We will set the mistletoe at the door of our house and decorate the boughs—not only to keep us from harm as you have prescribed but, at this season in particular, to remind us of our love for each other."

The Ancestors nodded. "Well done. You are a worthy partner for the Grand Master, especially *this* Grand Master."

Max put his arm around her. "I will guard

her well and love her more."

"It's time you returned." The Ancestors stepped back to the stones and spoke in one voice,

"As above, so below,
As within, so without.
Guidance and love they did obtain,
And bring a good year to their clan again."

ꙮ

Max and Ellyn firmly held on to the glowing staff. The wind swirled and blew around them. The storm ended as quickly as it began. When it cleared they stood at the great oak in Avebury. All the clans were close by staring as the great shadow moved and once again revealed the moon.

"Welcome." Doward came up and greeted them.

"The Grand Master is back." The people gathered around them. Max raised the staff for their attention.

"We have come back from the Ancestors. They bless us for another year. Their guidance is of love and understanding." Doward handed Max the golden scythe to cut fresh mistletoe off the great oak. Ellyn and the other women caught the delicate sprigs in a cloth they held under the oak's branches. The families took the mistletoe and went off to prepare for the evening's celebration.

"They set off rather quickly," said Max with Ellyn at his side.

"They have been planning the celebration for some time." Doward followed Max's darting gaze. "For whom are you looking?" Doward asked.

Max creased his brow. "Fendrel. I have

some news for him he may find distressing. Ah, there he is." He walked over to where Fendrel and his clan stood.

"Grand Master, it is good to have you back." He drew his wife in front of him. "This is my wife, Dimia, and our new son," he said, his chest puffed out with pride.

"Good eve to you, Dimia." He stroked the back of the infant's hand. The baby grabbed his finger. Max turned his attention to the new parents. "May you and your clan be blessed with good health and a full hearth."

"Thank you, Grand Master." Fendrel beamed.

"Fendrel, there is something we need to discuss," said Max.

"Yes, what it is?" Fendrel gave Dimia a sly smile.

Max put his arm protectively around Ellyn. "We are to be married."

Fendrel and Dimia looked at each other. Both exploded into wide smiles. "Yes, we know. We've been preparing ever since you left. You aren't the only one gifted with foresight."

"Do you also know your son's destiny?" asked Ellyn. When she peeked at the babe she saw the man he would become, a strong leader and a great druid knight. He would make Dimia and Fendrel proud.

Speechless, a startled expression set on the new parents' faces.

Ellyn looked at the wide-awake baby. "Our families will be forever tied to each other by our children. Our daughter and your son…"

"Arik. We've decided to name him Arik."

Dimia kissed the baby's head. "My little lion."

"Arik will continue our families," said Ellyn.

Fendrel stared at Max in disbelief. "Is it true?"

"If Ellyn says our families will be tied together by our children it must be so. Come, it is time to celebrate our good fortune and our future."

Max, with Fendrel and Dimia, set out for the great bonfire.

Ellyn and Doward followed behind.

"You knew, didn't you?" She waited but a heartbeat. "You made certain where I stood and when the portal opened you wished me a safe journey."

"I knew once you spent time together and learned to depend on each other you both would make the right decision. Ellyn, I know you and Max are to face challenges in the future. I will be there, always," Doward voiced with quiet determination.

"Thank you, Doward." She placed her hand on his arm. "We appreciate your devotion and friendship."

"I cannot change what is fated but I will do what I can—"

"That is more than anyone could ask." There was nothing she could do about the future. It would unfold as it was destined. Unless…she shaped it. Gave it direction. Knowing what the future held allowed them to prepare for it. Every moment was precious and she would make every one count.

She saw Max up ahead and her chest squeezed tighter with pride and love. He was her heart and together they could face anything. She glanced at Doward beside her. With a friend like him maybe the three of them could shape their destiny rather than be at its mercy. It might take a lifetime but something inside her said it was worth a try. They caught up to Max and the others.

The Grand Master stood before the bonfire and removed his tunic for everyone to see the sacred runes tattooed across his back. He picked up a lit branch. With his other arm he gathered Ellyn to his side. She ran her hand down his back, which made his muscles flinch and his tattoos softly glow.

He bent to her ear. "The runes warm to your touch."

"Perhaps it is a sign we are truly soul mates." She kept her eyes forward.

The sign. Of course. He smiled and raised the torch. "Is there anything else you want to tell me?"

"Her name will be Rebeka." She stared straight ahead, not meeting his eyes.

"Who?" he asked, a startled expression spread across his face.

"Our daughter. Arik's soul mate." A satisfied smile played on Ellyn's lips.

"She will be a mighty woman," he teased.

She looked into his eyes. "She will be the best of both of us. Now, finish the ritual. We have important things to…celebrate." She stepped aside and planted her staff deep into the ground between them.

He covered her hand with his. The staff glowed but only for them.

"Hail, Guardians, we thank you for the power of air, fire, water, and earth."

"For all you have given to us, we thank you

for the year," the congregation replied.

"For the new year we make this oath. We pledge ourselves to the Guardians, the Ancestors," he looked down at Ellyn, "and to each other. May our hearths and homes be safe and strong for another year."

"For all you offer us, we give thanks for the year to come."

He tossed the torch onto the pile and listened to the people shout with enthusiasm. He gathered Ellyn into his arms. "To hearth and home, my love."

They sealed their pledge with a kiss.

About…

Ruth started reading romance books while traveling the world for business. Traveling alone can be daunting but she found a book in hand could see her through long waits at the airport as well as being good company at dinner for one. For some of her longer treks, she pared down what she packed to make room for books. Her favorite genres are romance and adventure.

A seasoned professional with more than twenty-five years of writing experience in communications and marketing for a large financial institution, she gave way to her inner muse and began writing a series of historical fantasy romance novels. Ruth is published by Carina Press and Harlequin Books.

When not writing you can find her home in Teaneck, New Jersey, reading, cooking, doing Sudoku and counted cross-stitch. Together with her husband, Paul, they enjoy ballroom dancing and going to the theater. Ruth and Paul have three grown children and two grandchildren. They all thrive on spending time together. It's certainly a lively dinner table and they wouldn't change it for the world.

You can read more about Ruth online at
www.RuthACasie.com, on Twitter at
twitter.com/RuthACasie, or on Facebook at
www.facebook.com/RuthACasie.

Want to read more about Max and Ellyn's daughter, Rebeka, and Fendrel and Dimia's son, Arik? Look no further than ***Knight of Runes***, available now! www.RuthACasie.com/books.html

## *Knight of Runes*

*England, 1605*

When Lord Arik, a druid knight, finds Rebeka Tyler wandering his lands without protection, he swears to keep her safe. But Rebeka can take care of herself. When Arik sees her clash with a group of attackers using a strange fighting style, he's intrigued.

Rebeka is no ordinary seventeenth-century woman—she's traveled back from the year 2011, and she desperately wants to return to her own time. She poses as a scholar sent by the king to find out what's killing Arik's land. But as she works to decode the ancient runes that are the key to solving this mystery and sending her home, she finds herself drawn to the charismatic and powerful Arik.

As Arik and Rebeka fall in love, someone in Arik's household schemes to keep them apart, and a dark druid with a grudge prepares his revenge. Soon Rebeka will have to decide whether to return to the future or trust Arik with the secret of her time travel and her heart.

In the mood for more paranormal romance by Ruth A. Casie? Check out her latest story, ***The Guardian's Witch***, available now! www.RuthACasie.com/books.html

## *The Guardian's Witch*

*England, 1290*

Lord Alex Stelton can't resist a challenge, especially one with a prize like this: protect a castle on the Scottish border for a year, and it's his. Desperate for land of his own, he'll do anything to win the estate—even enter a proxy marriage to Lady Lisbeth Reynolds, the rumored witch who lives there.

Feared and scorned for her second sight, Lisbeth swore she'd never marry, but she is drawn to the handsome, confident Alex. She sees great love with him but fears what he would think of her gift and her visions of a traitor in their midst.

Despite his own vow never to fall in love, Alex can't get the alluring Lisbeth out of his mind and is driven to protect her when attacks begin on the border. But as her visions of danger intensify, Lisbeth knows it is she who must protect him. Realizing they'll secure their future only by facing the threat together, she must choose between keeping her magic a secret and losing the man she loves.

# Christmas Spirits

Lita Harris

Another Christmas keeps Emily Chadwick busy in the kitchen until her granddaughter discovers an ornament that has been hidden away along with memories from her grandmother's past. Emily opens her heart and tells her granddaughter about the grandfather she never knew. This Christmas brings something a bit more special than cookies.

Dedicated to ~

My partners for their unwavering support, encouragement, and understanding the importance of chocolate.

My husband, who supports me in whatever crazy idea that pops into my head.

Mallory Braus, for her keen editorial eye and guidance. You made this easy. Well, easier.

# Christmas Spirits
## by Lita Harris

"What's this, Grams?"

Emily Chadwick watched Olivia's tiny feet shuffle across the kitchen floor as she approached with a small globe nestled in her hands. She stood back from the stove and brushed a lock of frizzy bang away from her eyes. The beef stew was nearly ready as meat, carrots, onions, and potatoes simmered, a perfect winter meal. She flicked the back of her hand and Olivia stepped away from the stove.

"What do you have there?" She pulled out a hand-carved chair from the kitchen table—always meaning to replace them with something lighter and modern—but she couldn't bring herself to rid the house of any furniture Michael had made. She stretched out her arm as her granddaughter placed the piece of glass into her withered hands.

"Huh." Emily caught her breath. "Where did you find this?"

"In the attic. I was looking for Cleo. She ran

up there when I opened the door to let some cool air into the hallway upstairs."

The heat was difficult to control in the house, built in 1850, and the attic door proved more efficient at controlling the heat than a thermostat.

Emily held the ornament to the light. Snow filled the globe as she twirled it between her fingers. "Your grandfather made this when we first met."

"It's pretty." Olivia squinted her eyes. "Is that you and Grandpa on the lake?"

Emily nodded. "Yes it is. He was a stickler for detail. He didn't make much blown glass so this is very special. He focused mainly on furniture." She fought back a frown as she glanced at the silent guitar in the corner next to a chair by the kitchen fireplace.

Olivia stood back, away from the table, and clasped her hands behind her back. "I'm not touching it ever!"

"You'll have to at some point because it'll be yours." She laughed.

"Nope, give it to Mom."

Emily knew her granddaughter couldn't appreciate the sentimental value the ornament possessed, but she could tell Olivia knew it would be a bad thing if the ornament broke.

"You look sad, Grams."

She walked over to the sink and opened the window. Dust flitted through the room as the cool outside air merged with the heat from the kitchen fireplace. It was a constant battle to create a comfortable temperature in the old house. "Sit down, dear."

She strolled over to the kitchen table and pushed a plate of fudge walnut brownies toward her granddaughter. Olivia poured them each a glass of milk. Emily wrinkled her nose in silent protest but couldn't refuse the gesture. It was good for her, no matter how much she hated the taste and smell of milk.

Emily watched Olivia scoff down a brownie quicker than she could say the word. She enjoyed the time spent alone with her granddaughter. Soon, the day would come when Olivia wouldn't want to spend time at her grandmother's house to help bake Christmas cookies. Emily had seen it happen with her own daughter and she doubted that Olivia would be any different.

It had been years since she'd made a holiday dinner but every year she insisted on baking. It helped to keep her mind busy and not miss Michael so much.

"I wish you could have known your grandfather." She turned the ornament to catch the light. Fake snow swirled about the skaters on the lake.

"Mom talks about Grandpa a lot. I know she misses him." Olivia snatched another brownie.

Emily smiled. "I bet she does. All she ever had to do was ask for something and he jumped to help her." She picked up a brownie and nibbled the edge of the crusty confection. "That was his way. Always eager to help someone." *And that's how he died.* She closed her eyes and remembered that day.

Michael just *had* to go out into the blizzard and pull his buddy out of a ditch. But that's how he was. No one anticipated the cable line snapping and knocking him down the hill into a cluster of trees.

She couldn't be mad even though she missed him. He was doing what had made her fall in love with him, being generous, kind, and giving. She pushed the memory aside and sighed a deep breath of relief.

"I would have liked to meet him." Olivia took another brownie from the plate and shoved it into her mouth. "Tell me about him."

Emily swept her hand through the air, then pointed about the room. "Your grandfather bought this house for me and restored it himself right after we got married. He made nearly every piece of wood furniture that fills the rooms of this old place."

Emily picked up the ornament and cupped it in her hands. "But it was what he did before our wedding day that took my breath away and stole my heart forever." Tears filled her eyes.

"What was that, Grams?" Olivia knelt on the kitchen chair and her ten-year-old face glowed with excitement.

"Well, it all started in the late '60s…"

Emily Brody trembled on the thin blades of metal strapped to her feet as her best friend walked her onto the ice. The first and last time she'd been on ice skates was for a community benefit eight years ago. She hadn't done much better then, either.

"Do you think he'll be here?" Susan skated in a small circle.

"How would I know?" Emily called out as she steadied herself against the park bench perched alongside the frozen lake. But Susan was in love with Michael Chadwick and someone had told her that he skated at the lake every Sunday morning. So

Emily agreed to go ice-skating. Who was she to deny her best friend a chance at love?

Susan was boy-crazy and Emily couldn't be bothered with the immature boys in her school. That awkward social interaction came to an end when she graduated a few months ago, and she was fine with that.

She rested one hand on the bench while the other kept warm in her coat pocket. She did everything she could to keep her knees from knocking and her feet from sliding out from under her.

"Come on." Susan darted past her while she waited for an opening, not trusting her ability to dash out into the crowd. The last time she did that she collided with an old man who ended up in the hospital. She tightened her ankles a little too much, causing her knees to lock in place. A little girl no more than five spun in a circle in the center of the lake. That was enough to get Emily on the ice. Susan skated past her again. "Come on."

Emily removed her hand from the comfort of her pocket and held it out as if to hold back the onslaught of skaters whizzing past. *Whoosh! Whoosh!* It was him, the person Susan had dragged her out to see at an ungodly hour on a Sunday morning. Susan had pointed Michael out to her once when they were at the store. Emily thought he was cute and remembered him. She stepped back onto the grass to steady herself. Susan spun to a stop.

"Did you see him?" Susan cocked her hat.

"Yes. I couldn't help it since he nearly knocked me on the ground." She didn't like crowds because they made her feel claustrophobic. The lake was the only attraction in her small town and it was always crowded. The boaters and swimmers in the summer made it uncomfortable and you would think that ice-skating was the only thing to do in New Bedford in the winter. "I'm going to sit on the sidelines. Go do whatever you want." She waved the back of her hand to Susan.

"No." Her friend grabbed her arms and pulled her onto the ice.

"Stop it!"

"No! Let's go."

She didn't resist. There wasn't any time. Susan was that quick.

"I'll stay with you until you get your skating legs."

Emily gripped her best friend's hand. She trusted her. That was the thing about Susan—she was loyal and always came through when the situation was serious. Well, almost always.

It took only a few runs around the lake to get her bearings. The group of skaters didn't seem as chaotic once she was in the flow, and she relaxed into her body and found her rhythm.

"I'm going to let you go now. You okay?" Susan skated backward and turned to Emily.

She nodded. "I'm fine. Go off and find your true love." Emily started to extend her arm in her dramatic way but caught herself. She wasn't as steady as she'd thought.

Susan stopped.

"Go on, I'm fine. Just a little overconfident." She skated to the side with the other awkward skaters.

"You're sure?" Susan loosened her grip.

"I'm sure." Emily knew Susan would never let anything bad happen to her. They loved each other like sisters. Friends since Susan moved to town and she couldn't remember a day they hadn't been together.

"Yes, seriously. I'm fine."

"Okay then, you're on your own." Susan skated away with the confidence of an Olympic champion.

*Whoosh! Whoosh!* Emily hunched her shoulders with each blast of wind that hit her back. She looked for a break in the flurry of skaters as the activity overwhelmed her. She wanted to get out farther onto the ice and was sure that even the most inept skaters were now staring at her. She closed her eyes and took a deep breath. *I can do this. I can do this.* She was ready. She tightened her legs and shot out onto the ice.

"Ow! What the hell?" She landed flat on her back with her ankle tangled under her knee.

"I'm sorry." Michael reached out to her. "I hope I didn't hurt you." His voice was soft with concern.

"What happened?" She covered her eyes with her gloved hand to block out the sun.

"You cut me off." Michael bent down farther to help her, his voice even softer.

"I don't think so." She waved his hand away and tried to stand on her own. "Ow! Ow! Ow!"

Susan stopped short, her blades spraying ice into the air. "What happened?"

"He knocked me down." Emily pointed a shaky finger to Michael.

"I didn't. She cut me off. Darted right out onto the lake without looking." He leaned down to help her but she brushed him off. She grabbed on to Susan who ignored her gesture.

"Hi. I've seen you around town. My name's Susan. Yours?" Her voice was almost lyrical.

"Are you kidding me? Help." Emily smacked Susan in the leg. "Do you mind?" That was the thing about Susan—she was a good friend unless there was a guy involved. Emily never let herself get distracted by such trivial things because she didn't have the patience or time. Her butt was cold and her ankle swelled as if it was going to burst through her skate boot.

Michael skated behind Emily and slid his hands under her arms. "Ready?"

She nodded and gritted her teeth.

He slowly pulled her up to his chest.

"Stop…stop…stop!" She ripped her arms away from Michael. Pain shot up her left leg as she slid back onto the ice. Her breath shortened as a crowd gathered around them and the air closed in around her.

"What's the matter?" Susan rushed to her friend and knelt down beside her.

"I think my ankle is broken. I can't move it. It hurts." She tried to sit up straight but cringed with each movement as her ankle throbbed.

The crowd cleared the way for the ambulance driver as he wheeled a stretcher out onto the ice. "Move away please." A second emergency worker joined the rescue effort.

"Can you move on your own?" the driver asked.

"No. It hurts too much to breathe at this point." She tried to lean forward to unlace her skate but couldn't. Her butt neared numbness and embarrassment crept into her face. She didn't want to go skating in the first place but she had. This would be the last time she did something against her will. Trust your instincts—that's what her mother had always told her. No matter what someone else has planned for you—trust your instincts. Smart woman, her mother.

She flinched as the ambulance driver stabilized her ankle with a splint. She couldn't tell which was worse, the cold or the pain. The two men moved her onto the stretcher. The crowd spread out and made a path leading to the ambulance. Emily grabbed Susan by her coat collar. "I'm never going ice-skating again."

ꕥ

"Well, it looks like you got lucky." The doctor shoved the X-ray on the light board. "It's not broken but you have one serious soft tissue injury." His finger traced the bones in the image to show that nothing was broken. "Don't worry, you'll be able to go skating in about two months, though I suggest keeping those camel spins to a minimum."

Emily sighed. At least she wouldn't have the inconvenience of walking around with a cast on her leg in the middle of winter, or anytime for that matter. She remembered when her grandfather was in an arm cast for nearly two months and all he did was complain. She couldn't imagine having her leg restricted.

A knock on the door caught her attention and Michael poked in his head. "Can I come in?"

The doctor looked at her for approval.

"Sure." She waved him in. "I'm in the best place I can be if you want to do me in completely." Emily forced a slight smile. The least she could do was be somewhat forgiving since her leg wasn't a complete disaster.

"How is it?" Michael asked the doctor.

"Just a serious sprain. She'll need to stay off of it for a while."

Another knock on the door.

"Jeez, what is this place?" Emily turned to the doctor.

The door opened. The name tag introduced the orderly as Matthew. "I heard you were involved in an accident. You okay?" He patted Michael on the shoulder.

The blue scrubs and badge told Emily he worked there but she really didn't care at the moment. All she wanted to do was get home to bed and toss down whatever painkillers the doctor was going to give her.

"I'm fine. She's the victim."

She smiled. "Thanks for admitting that. You were doing your best to make it out to be my fault." She gave him a thumbs-up. "It's nice to know there are people who take responsibility for their actions."

"I was going to say, she was the victim of her own ignorance." Michael smirked.

"What?" She nearly jumped off the exam table while the doctor wrapped up her ankle. "What a crock—"

"Whoa, steady there." Matthew grabbed her hand to keep her on the table. "You can't be jumping around like that."

The door flung open again. "I called your parents and they're coming to pick you up." Susan walked up to Matthew. "Who are you?" She tapped her finger against her chin and then pointed to Michael. "You look like him."

"Yeah, we get that a lot. Twins, actually. Can you guess which one of us is older?" Michael challenged her.

Emily folded her arms across her chest. "Um, I really don't care and I doubt the hospital wants us to tie up their ER with a social event." She shuffled her legs. The swelled ankle pounded and she thought it would explode. She wanted to get home and pop some painkillers, elevate her ankle, and sink into a Cary Grant movie. That was her dream man—a bit old but her target date had to have the potential.

"Keep that foot elevated." The doctor left the examination room.

Matthew adjusted the pillow under her foot. "Just be patient and wait for your release."

"Aren't you a little young for this job?" Susan held his chin between her thumb and forefinger.

"Susan!" Emily rolled her eyes. She was embarrassed by her friend about as much as she loved her. Susan was infuriating at times but her heart was always in the right place even if she was inappropriate.

"I'm on a work-study program. I get to work a few hours a week to earn credits for college. It'll help me get through school faster. Let me check on your friend's discharge." Matthew smiled at Susan, not at all offended by her question.

Susan waited for Matthew and Michael to leave the room. "He's cute."

"Which one? You're kind of leaving Michael in the background." Emily squirmed.

"Matthew. He's really cute."

"They're identical twins; there's no

difference."

"Ah, but that's where you're wrong. Didn't you see Matthew's birthmark near his left ear?"

Emily hiked herself into a higher sitting position on the exam table. "Noooo, because I'm in pain!" A heavy sigh escaped her chest. "I could really care less about our social lives at the moment." She yanked on the sheet and covered her legs. "I just want to get home. Please go check on my parents." The commotion in her room and wait to leave the hospital frustrated her.

Susan quickly stepped back. "Will do." She opened the door just enough to slide out.

No sooner did the door close than it opened slightly. Michael peeked into the room. "I want you to know it was an accident."

Emily knew it was and she also knew it was mainly her fault. He seemed sincere to her. She took a deep breath. "You're forgiven." She ran her hand down to the throbbing bulge at the end of her leg. "I promise I'll do better next time before I dart out onto the ice."

He nodded. "And I promise to not skate so fast and close to the edge." He looked to the floor. "The truth is—"

"I can't hear you while you're talking into the floor." She lowered her head and turned her face so she could see his.

"The truth is I wanted to meet you."

"By plowing me down? That doesn't impress me much." She fought back a laugh. He was cute but he belonged to Susan even if she also showed interest in Matthew. Emily would never assume it was okay to flirt with Michael.

He lifted his head and stood straighter. With

his coat off, she could see the muscular outline of his chest. His dark, wavy hair hung casually over his left eye. She strained to see if he had a birthmark over his left ear. Hmm…no, nothing there. No identifying mark. He was perfect. That was one way she would be able to tell them apart. She did notice that Michael's hair was a bit longer than his brother's but that could easily change.

He stepped into the room but held the door open behind him. "The way I see it is, the only way to get past this is to take you to dinner. It's not an admission of guilt but it might be nice to see if we can laugh about this as your ankle heals."

She froze for a moment. There was no way she could do that to her best friend. Susan was the reason they were at the lake. Michael was the reason Susan had brought them there. She rested her arm against her stomach to quell the somersault making her queasy. "I would love to go but I can't."

He walked closer to her, the door closing behind him. "Of course you can. It's not like you'll be able to get around much. I'll pick you up for dinner next Saturday. It'll give you a week to heal."

"I really can't." She lowered her head and thought about Susan. How could she accept a date from Michael? It would be like betraying her sister. Even though Susan came across as unfeeling at times, that was how she protected herself from heartache. Emily could never hurt her friend. How could this be happening? It wasn't like she sent out any signals to him. If anything, she had been rude. Yet she couldn't help but wonder what a dinner alone with him would be like.

Susan flung the door open and barged into the room. "Your parents are here in the lobby.

What's this about next Saturday?" Susan crossed her arms across her chest. She cocked her head toward Michael but her eyes were settled on Emily.

"I want to take her to dinner next Saturday to beg forgiveness but she turned me down." He glanced at Emily.

"Humph, as she should." Susan threw her arms open, walked over to Emily, and hugged her.

"That's what best friends do." Emily smiled. Would Susan have done the same? Their friendship had never been tested on the boyfriend front. Clothes and records were easy. Yes, this was different. The conversation was too serious for Emily and she wanted to hide under the bed.

ꕤ

The three flights of steps were difficult to manage with crutches and she found it easier to pull herself up the winding banister.

Emily climbed into her bed as best she could with the help of her mother. Her little brother had her bedding pulled back and pillows piled up for her to rest her ankle. He wasn't so annoying right now. Ever since he'd realized she was leaving for college he started doing little things to please her. He probably wanted to earn points toward getting her room once she left for school.

"It's a good thing you put off starting college for a semester. Hobbling around the college campus would be difficult." Her mother tucked in the bed covers around Emily's legs.

"Thanks, Mom."

Her mother left the room. Emily rubbed the back of her neck. All her mother ever talked about was Emily going away to college. It was never a question of Emily not going to college but what she would do with it. She took off the first semester to give herself time to be with her mother and to take a break from school.

She turned on the TV for background noise. The pain meds were kicking in and her body floated like she was on a cloud. It was weird. She had never taken anything stronger than an aspirin. Her entire leg was hurting, not just her ankle, and she wasn't out to prove how tough she was. The weather lady told her a snow storm was coming. Nothing new for New Bedford. Winters were always expect the unexpected, wear plenty of layers and you're good. That's probably why she didn't break her leg. She'd been wearing enough wool, cotton, and whatever else her wardrobe was made of, to fend off an army.

Even an army of one…

"Hmm, Michael," she whispered as she drifted off to sleep.

A loud bang on the door stirred her from her painkiller-induced sleep. Her head lay heavy on the pillow. "Come in," she barely whispered.

Susan stormed in with a potted poinsettia and plopped it on the windowsill.

Emily stirred and pulled the cover up to her neck. "I hate those plants."

"Too bad. That's all the store had for a get-well flower. I figure it'll be dead before you can climb out of bed to take care of it anyway. It does look kind of sad."

"Half price?" Emily forced a smile.

"Of course." Susan held out her arms and took a bow.

One quality that bound them as friends was

their ability to find good deals. They would laugh at their former schoolmates that spent ridiculous amounts of money on celebrity-endorsed clothing. Emily and Susan had goals. Emily was going to college and determined to not repeat her mother's life path. Not that she was embarrassed by her mother, but she wanted more. She never wanted to rely on a man for support.

Susan…well, her goal was a little different. She did want to marry, but she wanted to marry well. Her reason for going to college was to find a wealthy husband so she wouldn't have to worry about money. She had lived in a trailer park when she was a little girl and she swore she would never be in that situation again.

Emily patted the bed but her hand, heavy from medication, slipped off the edge of the mattress. "Sit. I may not be much company. Pills kicked in."

Susan gently sat on the edge of the bed then carefully slid her legs up onto the mattress and lay next to Emily. She rested her hand on Emily's shoulder. "Do you realize that we're going away to school in a few weeks?"

"Uh-huh," Emily muttered.

"Today made me realize what that means. The little bit of time we have left to spend together. One more Christmas." Susan leaned down to Emily's ear. "I'm invited for dinner, right?"

"Yes, yes. Always welcome." Emily shifted her weight and pushed Susan's hand from her forehead. The medication made it feel like she was being pushed underwater.

"I didn't plan on spending our last few weeks holed up in your bedroom watching… Why the hell are you watching the weather station?" Susan picked up the remote and changed the channel to *Bewitched.* "I don't plan on letting you sleep through the next few weeks so I'm here to tell you that we're going to dinner next Saturday."

Emily tried to open her eyes, but they were too heavy from the medication. She saw Michael in her mind's eye. "Why?"

"We're going to dinner with the boys. Michael and Matthew. I think they're a bit pretentious using their formal names. I called Michael, Mike, and he nearly bit my head off."

Emily rolled over to face Susan. "You don't like anyone calling you Sue."

"Whatever. Anyway, we are going to dinner with them on Saturday. I figured it'll be the perfect opportunity to get to know Michael."

"Why don't you just go together?" All she wanted to do was sleep. It was getting harder to keep this conversation going, one that she had no interest in because the pills made her not care.

Susan shifted and crossed her arms. "I tried that. He wants you to go, something about feeling guilty. So give him this one so he can sleep at night and I can move on with getting to know him better." She gently prodded Emily with her elbow.

Emily's eyes fluttered to stay open. She rolled her head to her best friend who was annoying her with the nonstop talk about a dinner she didn't care about. She wanted sleep—uninterrupted sleep. "I'll go if you leave. Leave and don't come back until I call you and tell you it's okay to come here."

Susan stood up from the bed and spoke softly. "Will it be before Christmas dinner?"

"Leave." Emily threw her arm across the

bed and pointed at the door.

"Love ya. Get better fast."

ℵ

Emily wrapped her hands around her knee and hoisted her leg out of the car. It had been a week since she'd left the house. The snowstorm had been enough to keep her inside and not risk another accident. Even tonight she didn't want to go, but she promised Susan they would have dinner with Michael and Matthew. At least they were going to her favorite Italian restaurant. Her pain had abated so she didn't need any more painkillers and could have an intelligent conversation not riddled with meds.

"Here, let me help." Michael snuck up behind Emily as she got out of the car.

She grabbed the top of the car door to keep herself from slipping. "You scared me. Do you have some sort of weird vendetta against me?" Emily held back a smile. She was happy to see him but didn't want to seem too eager. The last thing she wanted was her friendship with Susan to be torn apart by someone they barely knew. "Here, take this." She handed a crutch to Michael while she used her other one to prop herself up. She waited for Susan to come around and get her.

The restaurant was empty except for two tables, but it was early. Susan made sure there would be enough time to get to know Michael. Emily took her crutch from him.

"We'll sit here." Susan pulled out a chair for Emily.

She glanced at Michael when he stood back

as the girls settled into their seats. She could tell he was a few years older than her by the way he carried himself. He didn't slouch like most guys in their teens and she could see evidence of a beard and mustache aching to surface.

"I hear this is a great place to eat." He took his seat after Emily settled in.

"You've never been here?" Susan slowly removed a bread stick from the basket and held it playfully between her fingers.

"No, I haven't. I don't eat out much." He turned to Emily. "That was another reason I wanted to ask you out."

She looked at Susan and pleaded with her eyes that she had nothing to do with Michael paying so much attention to her. She wanted to crawl under the table. Most of her school life was uneventful. Invisible, that's how she always felt. It wasn't until Susan moved to New Bedford and befriended Emily that she had any type of social life. Her plan was to graduate and go to college—and she was nearly there. The last thing she needed was to get involved with a boyfriend or something else to distract her from her life plan.

"You know, I've already told you that it was nothing. It's not like my leg is broken. A few more weeks and it will be like nothing happened. You can forget about me, like we never even met." Emily grabbed a bread stick and shoved it in her mouth. She leaned back hard and the chair smacked against the wall.

"You know, Michael, Emily is going away to school in a few weeks." Susan twirled her hair.

"Really? What school?" Michael stretched his arm across the top of the empty chair.

"No place special," Emily mumbled through her bread stick.

"But it is far, far away." Susan waved her hand through the air. Her desperate attempts to hold Michael's attention were lost on him.

Emily picked up the menu and read it like it required intense scrutiny. Anything to deflect the conversation away from her. She was never comfortable being the center of attention. Not that she ever really was, which was probably why she didn't like it. "Shrimp scampi. That's all I want." She put down the menu just as the waitress walked up to the table.

"Um, a few more minutes. We're waiting for someone." Michael held up his palm to stop the waitress from taking their orders. "I hear college is nice. I've never been."

Susan choked on her bread. "Never? Why not?"

"Never had a desire to go and doubt I ever will." He took a bread stick and propped his elbow on the table as he stared at her like he was challenging her to an academic war. "Ah, there he is."

Matthew slumped down into the last empty chair. "What a night." He was still dressed in his scrubs from the emergency room.

"You need to sleep more." Michael winked at his brother.

"I know. Good evening, ladies. Sorry I'm late." Matthew pulled off his jacket and placed it on the back of his chair. If Emily didn't know better she would have sworn that Matthew was the older brother. He had a more serious and professional presence about him. Now, Michael, he didn't seem to take too much seriously. His eyes drilled into her soul when he looked at her. It made her feel uncomfortable yet intrigued. But she had to push that aside. Tonight was the perfect opportunity for Susan but Emily wanted to know more about Michael.

"Work a lot, do you?" Susan leaned across the table to Matthew.

He ran his fingers through his hair. "Have been lately. Always more so around the holidays."

"Why's that?" Susan narrowed her eyes, seeming genuinely interested in Matthew.

"Who knows? Bad weather, people drink more. It's dark most of the day." He sat back in the chair, arms folded across his chest.

Michael glanced at Emily who wasn't up for conversation. She was just glad to be out of the house. She didn't want to interrupt the exchange between Matthew and Susan who seemed to have forgotten all about Michael. That was typical of Susan. Fickle. Emily moved her leg closer to the fireplace. The heat felt good on her ankle and she could sit there all night basking in its warmth.

The waitress approached the table. "Can I take your order now?"

"Yes, thank you." Emily perked up, starved and glad for the distraction. "I'll have lobster ravioli with the Alfredo sauce."

"No scampi?" Michael asked.

"Nope, changed my mind." She handed the menu to the waitress.

"Hmm, that sounds good. I'll have the same." Michael grabbed a bread stick and motioned to Emily.

"Ewww, not me. I hate fish." Susan crinkled

her nose. “Chicken parm with linguine on the side.”

“I’ll have what she’s having.” Matthew motioned to Susan. Then he leaned across the table and whispered to her, “I’m allergic to shellfish, which lobster is. It’s not fish.” He smiled and leaned back, not breaking his stare.

Emily suppressed a laugh. Susan didn’t like to be corrected but she would never get into a confrontation while trying to impress Michael.

“So, Michael, what do you do?” Susan grabbed a bread stick and snapped it in half, sending crumbs flying onto Matthew’s plate.

“Not much right now. Music mostly. I play drums or guitar whenever I can get a gig.” He spread his napkin across his lap as the waitress put down more bread. “My brother is the intellect in the family.”

Emily watched Susan’s jaw fall open. There was no way Susan would date a musician. No way. She wanted a stable relationship, steady income, and a modest but comfortable house to entertain people. Emily knew that Susan wasn’t going back to a trailer park and in her mind being a musician wasn’t far from that. Susan pursed her lips as she glanced over at Emily. *Sometimes you get what you want but most times you don’t.* That’s what Emily’s mother always told her, which is why her mother was adamant that Emily get herself settled in life and *then* find someone who could support her choices.

Susan turned her attention to Matthew. “So what do you do when you’re not cleaning the ER?”

The waitress placed their food on the table, getting the order right without any help.

Matthew turned to Susan, lowered his head,

and stared straight into her eyes without flinching. "I don't clean the emergency rooms. I'm going to be a doctor." He tapped his fork on the plate and stabbed his chicken Parmesan. He leaned back in his chair, chewing his food as he folded his arms across his chest, tilted his head, and stared at Susan.

"This smells delicious." Emily didn't care what Susan said and looked for any excuse to change the subject. She could tell that Michael was history as far as Susan was concerned. Emily knew that for sure and with that thought she smiled and looked at Michael. Maybe she could date just for a little bit before heading off to school.

ꕥ

She was down to one crutch and kind of missed using the other. Michael called a few times but she refused to take his calls. She needed to talk to Susan first, who had been gone for a few days to visit her father. Nothing much had been discussed about the dinner except for a quick mention that Michael didn't fit into Susan's life plan. Emily was happy that Susan lost interest in Michael because she found herself thinking about him all the time. Though they hadn't spoken much at dinner that night, Emily was attracted to Michael.

It wasn't unusual that Susan had nowhere to go for the holidays. Susan's stepmother didn't like her so she wouldn't stay at her father's house, and her mother was away at some commune in Florida. Being an only child had its advantages but it was lonely most of the time. She would feel Susan out later tonight since she was staying over.

"Mom, that smells great," Emily yelled as

she hobbled down the hallway stairs to the kitchen. "Loin of pork?" The smell of garlic filled the room.

It was a Brody tradition—her mother always made a meat dish with a lot of garlic for Christmas Eve. Something about cleansing the air for the good to enter the house, something Emily wasn't in total agreement with but it was her mom's house. One day she would have her own traditions.

"Yes, and it's almost done. Did Susan get here yet?" Her mother basted the rosemary-roasted potatoes cooking alongside the main course.

"On her way. She called from the gas station. She's just outside of town." Emily laid her crutch aside. "I'll set the dining room table."

"No need. Your brother did it."

"Okay." She made her way through to the living room, holding on to furniture to steady herself. She stopped to admire the Christmas tree. It was taller this year, not short and bushy like previous trees. She straightened hand-strung popcorn garland, made by her and her brother, draped along the branches. She would make sure to be home in time for the holidays to continue that tradition. She was a little sad about leaving her family. She rearranged a few closely placed candy canes while her brother wasn't looking.

"Hello." Susan stamped her feet in the vestibule to clean her snow-covered boots. "Here you go. An artificial wreath from my artificial stepmother." She placed the wreath round Emily's neck.

"Gee, thanks. I was wondering what to wear that would match my reindeer sweater." Emily laughed.

"Don't mention it." Susan kicked off her

boots and tossed her jacket on the hallway coatrack. "How's the foot?" She cupped Emily's arm and guided her to the couch.

"Fine. I've been treated like royalty. I may never leave."

"Oh, my queen, but you must!" Susan threw back her head and slapped the back of her hand against her forehead. "Your subjects await your degree in whatever it is you're going to major in."

Emily held her stomach as she laughed. "Education, my lady, education. So I can expand the minds of our youth."

"If you say so. I still haven't decided what I'm going to major in. My dad asked and I told him I'll figure it out. He told me he's only paying for the first two years of school. Some encouragement, huh?" she said sarcastically.

"Don't worry. It'll all work out." Now was the time to talk. "Um, have you heard from Michael?"

Susan pushed her headband in place and ran her fingers down through the flip of her hair. "No, and I don't think I want to."

Emily fought back a smile, not wanting to burst with happiness. "Why not?"

"He's a musician! That doesn't work into my plan at all. I'm not traveling all over the country living out of a bus."

"He's a session player. I doubt he travels much." Emily felt the need to defend him. She found his calling fascinating. Compared to the neighborhood boys, Michael was a man of the world. Much bigger than New Bedford.

"Okay, and there's that. How much local work can he possibly get? I'm not living off of beans again." Susan collapsed on the couch.

"Drama." Emily took a candy cane from the dish on the coffee table.

"Drama what?" Susan plopped her head on the armrest.

"You need to major in drama. You would be doing the public an injustice if you didn't follow your calling." Emily remembered Michael's soulful eyes. She couldn't avoid his calls any longer and she didn't want to.

"Dinner's ready." Her mother clapped her hands as the family gathered around the table. An admirer of Jackie Kennedy, her mother set the table in elegant style.

The doorbell rang. "I'll get it." Emily was slow getting to the table so she was the closest to the door. The hardwood floor and her socks made it easy for her to slide to the entryway. She peeked through the sidelight. No one was there. She opened the door just a bit to find a small box on the porch.

"What the…" She reached down for the box and then retreated. *What could it be?* She looked around and saw a set of footprints in the freshly fallen snow. She bent over the crudely wrapped box. *Emily, this is for you,* read a tag hanging from the twine around the box. She looked around again—nothing. She carefully pulled the twine bow and the brown paper unfolded. *Whoever wrapped this needs lessons.* She opened the flap and revealed a glass-blown ornament with two ice-skaters inside. "Oh my." She clasped her hand over her mouth. It was from Michael—she knew it was. The skaters looked like them the day they met.

Her heart raced as she covered it up and put it in the hall closet to join her family and Susan.

ຯଓ

"Finally, the last dish put away." Emily closed the cabinet door. She started to sit at the kitchen table but changed her mind and headed to the living room. After all, with the decorations surrounding them, how could Susan get mad with Santa staring at her from the fireplace mantel?

"Are you okay?" Susan reached out to Emily.

"I'm fine. But we need to talk. Sit." A huge sigh escaped Emily's lips as she made her way to the couch. "I've needed to talk to you since we went to dinner with Michael and Matthew."

Susan folded her arms. "And what do you have to talk about?"

Emily drew a silent breath and hugged her stomach. "What's the deal with you and Michael? I think I know but I want to be sure." She finally asked the question. It was finally out there in the open—waiting for an answer. Her stomach quivered in anticipation.

"Why? Do you know something?" Susan leaned forward, her elbow propped on her knee, chin in her hand.

"No, and that's why I'm asking. You were going crazy to meet him, then you did and you haven't said anything." Emily twirled a stray thread on her sweater. "I was simply wondering."

Susan narrowed her eyes. "Look at me, Emily Brody."

She looked away.

"I said look at me." Susan cupped Emily's chin and looked into her eyes. "I don't believe this. You like him."

"Susan, I didn't…I swear…I don't know what it is. But I do know that I cannot and will not get involved with him if it means ruining our friendship." She wrung her hands.

"Well, I never thought I would see this." Susan threw her head back and planted the back of her hand on her forehead.

Emily's stomach tightened. She never thought a guy would come between them. "I'm sorry. I didn't mean for it to happen." She fought back tears.

Susan stood up and walked toward the door. "I really don't know about this. I mean, you're my best friend."

Tears ran down Emily's cheek.

"Oh jeez, stop bawling. Don't you know me by now?" Susan smiled and ran over to Emily and hugged her tight. "I think it's fantastic that you finally found someone. I can't believe you didn't say something sooner."

Emily wiped her nose with the sleeve of her sweater. "I figured that night at dinner that it didn't go so well but you never said anything. As soon as he said he was a musician I knew he was off your list."

"Then you do know me as well as you should." Susan pulled Emily close and kissed her on the crown of her head. "You have my blessing." She grabbed a candy cane from the tree. "But I never would have guessed he would be your type."

Emily smiled without guilt for the first time in a week. She may have confessed to Susan about her feelings for Michael—well, in a roundabout way—but she was not going to tell her about the secret present hiding in the closet. That was only for her, for now anyway. *Merry Christmas to me.*

She refused to hang the ornament on the tree and kept it hidden in her room, taking it out of its crude box on a daily basis to admire it. It wasn't anyone's business and she especially didn't want Susan to know. At least not yet.

The letter inside the box mentioned Michael would be away for Christmas Day but he would call her when he got back, and he did. For the first time she felt special. Someone she liked was interested in her. She rushed to get ready for what would be her first real date, and with Susan's blessing. She wasn't sure what to wear. He said casual, but that could mean anything. Her mother thought casual was a patterned dress. She opted for black leggings and a cream-colored tunic sweater, which would be appropriate for just about anyplace he was going to take her.

It hadn't stopped snowing since Christmas Eve and that made New Bedford look like a Currier and Ives painting. Fresh snow blanketed the evergreens brilliant with lights. The pristine carpet of snowflakes created a calm over the town. Emily liked it best this time of year, a time when everyone took a moment to be a little nicer. She waited on the front porch for Michael to pull up—not that she didn't want him to meet her family but she wanted to embrace the evening and experience it for herself. What if she really liked him? She couldn't start a relationship and then take off. And what about him? He didn't know where his next job was going to be. Sometimes her practical nature got in the way of her enjoying life.

She clutched her jacket closed and sighed, watching ice crystals form from her breath. She leaned out and peered down the street.

Headlights appeared around the corner. The 1958 Impala slowed as it approached her house. *Hmm, not bad.* He rolled to a stop and reached across to open the door for her. *Okay, so he didn't get out to open the door.* "Punctual, I see." She slid into the warm leather seat. "This yours?"

"Yep. Got it as a graduated-from-high-school-going-to-college gift." He pulled away.

"But you said you're not going to college."

"Correct, and that's why I have to pay half of it off."

She sat back and watched him drive. His car was clean and he used turn signals. Did he come to a complete stop at lights? Most definitely. So far so good. She felt comfortable with him at the wheel, which was a good thing so she could relax. She wasn't the calmest passenger.

"Where are we going? You didn't say, so I wasn't sure how to dress." She tugged at her leggings to prove she had no clue.

"You're fine." He pulled into the parking lot at the lake. The ice reflected like a mirror. Not many people were skating and it was a beautiful night. He walked around to her door and opened it. He slid his hand into hers as they walked to the concession stand. "Hot dog?"

She smiled and tugged her hat farther down over her ears. "Quite different than Italian."

"I like to mix it up. Two dogs, mustard and relish, one fry, and a cola," he told the kid at the stand. "And what would you like?"

“Hmm. Two dogs, chili and onions, onion rings, and a ginger ale.” What if he wanted to kiss her? “You know what? Change that. I’ll have what he’s having but keep the ginger ale.”

A table freed up and she claimed it. Who knew so many people ate at the lake in winter?

He carried the food to their table and sat across from her. She’d hoped that he would sit next to her but at least this way she could see him better. *Hmm, what color are his eyes? Blue? Green?* They seemed to change color every time he moved his head toward the light. *Intriguing.* She picked up a hot dog—too hungry to be graceful, but still yearning for a mouthful of chili laced with onions.

“It’s a nice night.” He picked up his cola.

“And the snow tapered off just in time.” She picked at a French fry. “I’ve never eaten here. This is an interesting choice.”

“I thought it was a good place to start over since our first meeting was a little, well, rough.” He laughed. “How’s your foot?”

“My ankle? Much better. Won’t be doing any skating tonight.” She waved her hand toward the lake.

“That’s fine. They don’t allow skating in the movie theater anyway.” He finished his last hot dog.

“Movie?”

“Sure. Dinner and a movie. Isn’t that standard for a first date?” He wiped his mouth with a napkin.

“I guess.” She didn’t want to admit that she had never really been on a date before. She couldn’t take her eyes off of him. He seemed much older than her, mature and worldly. He wasn’t awkward like the schoolboys she was used to. Maybe it was the confidence he exuded or the fact that he wasn't from New Bedford. She didn't even know where he came from but she was sure it was a big city.

"Ready?" He held out his hand to her.

ꕥ

She didn't care much for the movie. At least it was a comedy and not one of those war pictures she disliked so much. It was getting late and she was tired. Her stomach was a tad queasy. The popcorn on top of hot dogs and French fries was a bit too much in one night. She didn't want to be bossy on their first date so she went along with what he had planned.

"How did you like it?" He draped his arm around her shoulder as they walked to his car.

"It had its moments." She could barely feel him through their heavy winter clothing and the scent of popcorn was beginning to dissipate in the cool air.

He opened the car door for her.

She quickly fumbled through her purse and found a piece of gum. The wrapper was melted to it but she popped it in her mouth anyway. She gave it one or two chews and spit it out before he got into the car. Why wasn't she better prepared? Hopefully he had his own gum.

"Are you from the area?" She really didn't care, but was uncomfortable with awkward silence. She noticed that he wasn't much of a talker. Which she kind of liked. She'd never noticed how little she talked. Susan yapped nonstop so Emily rarely had an opportunity to say much.

He pulled away slowly on the icy street.

"Boston until a few months ago."

"Hmm, I thought so." She turned to face him while he drove.

"Accent?"

"Surprisingly, no. I knew you weren't from around here, that's all." She looked out the windshield. Her legs tensed as the car crawled down the street. She loved her town but some winters could be harsh. He seemed to know what he was doing as he maneuvered the car down the slick pavement. She rested her fists in her coat pockets and tightened them against her body. She kept quiet until they were off the icy road, which fortunately wasn't too long.

"You can relax now." He smiled at her.

"What do you mean? I am relaxed." She unclenched her hands before pulling them out of her pockets.

"Okay. Whatever you say, but I can tell when someone is scared and your clenched teeth and hands gave you away."

"I was being polite. I didn't want to distract you." She turned back to him. "What brought your family here?"

He turned onto her street. Most houses still had Christmas lights lit since it was the day before New Year's Eve. Snowflakes started to fall again and she wanted him to get home before the weather got worse. That was the thing with New England, the weather pretty much dictated how you managed your day. The car rolled to a stop in front of her house.

"Father's job, then he got laid off."

She waited for a cue. Should she get out? No, she waited. He opened the car door for her at the lake and movie theater. He didn't turn off the car ignition so she grabbed the door handle. He jumped out of the car with it running and came around the front to her door and opened it. This was going well. She liked a gentleman. "After you." He held out his hand.

"Thank you." She got out of the car. "I had a great time."

He put his arm around her waist and walked her up the front stairs. "I'm glad."

She stopped at the door. The lights were off in the house except for the holiday lights. "Oh, I never thanked you for that ornament. Where did you get it?"

"Get it? I made it." He smiled.

"Really?" She stepped back, her eyes squinted as she tried to figure out if he was telling the truth.

"Really. Didn't you notice the two ice-skaters? They didn't look familiar?" He almost looked insulted.

"Of course I did but I thought you just happened upon something familiar. It's wonderful. The workmanship is amazing."

"Thank you. I'll take that as a compliment. My grandfather taught me how to blow glass and my father taught me how to carve. Both skills sadly falling out of favor." He bowed. "I was fortunate to learn them. My grandfather passed away and my father can't carve anymore because of his arthritis."

"What about your brother?"

"Nope. He decided to study books, not crafts."

She stepped in closer to him. "Well, I think it's lovely and I am honored to be the recipient of such a unique gift."

He wrapped his arms around her and pulled her close. "That's exactly how I feel now."

The wind kicked up a bit and she buried her face in his chest. His heart beat against her and she knew she was in the right place. Or was she? She closed her eyes and fought to push aside the words of her mother. *Go to school. Take care of yourself and then find happiness in someone.* What if she had found happiness first?

He tipped his head back and lifted her chin. His blue eyes burned into hers. His breath brushed her lips ever so slightly. Her shoulders slumped and her breathing quickened. His arms pulled her in tighter. She waited. Maybe her mother was wrong. His lips brushed hers and she welcomed him. His arms melted into her back. The cold air no longer embraced them. It was only them. He kissed her with force yet his lips were soft against hers. Her head grew light, as did her heart.

She slowly moved back and lowered her face into his chest again. She had never felt so comfortable. "I—I…"

"Shush. Have I made up for injuring you?" he said quietly.

"Most definitely." She hugged him.

He stepped back and slid his hands down to her elbows, holding her at arm's length. "I'm going to marry you one day."

He walked away.

She collapsed against the front door and turned to watch him get into the car. *He might be right.*

ꟸ

"And he did, didn't he, Grams?" Olivia hung on to every word as she knelt on a stool, elbows on the table with her chin resting on her fists.

"Yes, he did, sweetheart. Your grandpa was a determined man and he won my heart. I even became a better ice-skater." She slid the last batch of oatmeal raisin cookies from the sheet onto cooling racks. "You would have liked him." Emily handed a chocolate chip cookie to her granddaughter.

"That's what Mom says." Olivia took a bite of the cookie.

Emily picked up the ornament. "I think I have the perfect place for this." She walked over to the kitchen sink and hung the globe of memories from the planter of ivy perched in the window. "There's no reason why this can't be out all year."

"This way you can see it every day, Grams."

Emily suppressed a tear as she gently shook the winter scene. She could feel Michael next to her, like they were skating. They skated a few more times on the lake after her ankle healed and even after they'd married. He told her that first night he was going to marry her and four years later he did. Of course, after she graduated college. A month to the day.

Michael became a local celebrity as he shared his music with few. That was okay with him even though Emily encouraged him to pursue his dreams. He was content making furniture and playing the occasional gig.

She didn't want Olivia to see her crying. "Get your cookies together, dear. Your mother will be here soon."

Olivia grabbed the cookie box decorated

with snowmen, just as she had for the past three years, and piled it with at least a dozen of each: chocolate chip, oatmeal raisin, peanut butter, and shortbread. It was the one day a year they spent together, just the two of them. Each year more special than the last.

"What time are you coming for Christmas dinner?" Olivia finished boxing her cookies.

"The same time I always do. I'll be there at noon." She gathered her granddaughter's coat and hat and hugged her just as a car horn blew in the driveway. "How about that? Perfect timing."

Olivia put down the box of cookies and hung from Emily's neck as she hugged her goodbye. "Love you, Grams. See you in a few days."

"Bye, sweetheart." She walked to the front door and waved to her daughter as she watched Olivia climb into the car. They never discussed with anyone else what took place on baking day and for that reason Olivia's mother waited in the car. Baking day was for Emily and Olivia and whatever secrets were spoken were theirs alone.

The kitchen was nearly clean. A quick swipe of the island and a few cookie trays to wash would have her finished with baking for the season. She didn't enjoy it as much as she used to. If it weren't for Olivia she would have stopped baking years ago. Too tired to wash the rest of the dishes, she put them in the dishwasher, something she had fought Michael on when he remodeled the kitchen. She felt it didn't go with the period of the house. Dishwashers didn't exist in the 1800s but Michael insisted it be installed and she would learn to appreciate it one day. He was right again. He usually was, because he knew her better than she knew herself, but he never made her feel uncertain.

Yes, he usually was right about things because he made certain they worked out the way he planned. He was even sure that he would die first. She never wanted to believe that but once again he proved to be right. Her mother had been right, as well, and the past twenty years proved that. If it hadn't been for her teaching degree she never would have survived. The students had kept her busy but it was at home where the empty hours nagged her.

The sound of glass breaking came from the dishwasher. She turned it off and let the water settle. Shards of a drinking glass littered the inside. Tears rolled down her cheeks. "Oh, Michael. You would think I'd be okay after all these years." She ripped a paper towel from the holder and scooped up the splinters of glass. "It's times like this I really miss you." She laughed to herself as the tears fell. The crackling fire in the kitchen hearth kept her company most cool nights. Michael's handmade rocking chair sat still next to his silent guitar, which he used to play on cold nights as they sat by the fire.

The telephone rang and broke the silence. Emily turned the dishwasher back on and answered the phone. "Hello, dear." Her daughter called tonight as she always did since Michael passed away. "I have enough cookies to bring for Christmas dinner and she'll get sick if she eats too many." She nodded as she listened to her daughter. "Okay, dear. Yes, I know. Good night."

Tiredness overcame her. She looked at Michael's chair, which had not been sat in by anyone since he passed away. She pulled her shawl from the corner chair and walked over to the rocker. She tapped the bottom of the chair with her toe and set it in gentle motion. The empty chair rocked back and forth with a smooth, melodic rhythm.

It came to a halt. She sat down and ran her hands along the arms of the chair, the armrests that her husband had carved so many years ago. She would have to give his guitar to Olivia. Someone should enjoy it. He never made it big in music but his granddaughter should know how important it was to him.

Her eyes grew heavy as she pulled the blanket across her lap and folded her arms across her stomach. The dishwasher whirred and the fire gave spark to the occasional stray ember. Her eyes closed and her breathing grew shallow.

"Emily, dear." His whisper, just like she remembered.

She could hear him.

"Open your eyes, dear, it's time."

"Michael?"

"Come with me." His voice was peaceful and loving.

Her spirit rose from the chair as he reached out for her hand. He embraced her and slid his arm around her waist.

"It's okay." He walked her to the door and it opened before them. Skaters glided across the frozen lake but she wasn't cold. He held her close and she trusted him. "You're home."

About…

Lita Harris spends her time between New Jersey and the Endless Mountains region of Pennsylvania, where she writes most of her books. She also lived in Alaska for a short time just for fun. An avid crafter, unused supplies clutter her basement and attempts at making pottery, jewelry, and stained glass are proudly displayed in her house, usually behind a picture or holding a door open. She also makes candles and homemade soap. With enough books to stock a small library she may need to construct a building to store her literary obsessions.

She writes in multiple genres, including women's fiction, contemporary romance, paranormal, and cozy mysteries.

For more information about Lita, please visit her website at www.LitaHarris.com or at twitter.com/litaharris and facebook.com/litaharrisauthor.

For more stories by Lita Harris, try ***Love At Christmas,*** Available December 2013 from Sweet Cravings Publishing.

## Love at Christmas

Kristen Anderson is resigned to live a child-free life in New Jersey. That is, until she's given custody of her seven-year-old nephew after the death of his mother. Christmas brings them to their grandmother's house in Pennsylvania where the family focuses on healing and reopening the family inn in time for the holidays. Enter Luke Baldwin, a man with a past that leaves him uncertain whether he'll ever find love—until he meets Kristen.

Kristen's and Luke's desire to be together is complicated by Kristen's yearning to return to New Jersey, her grandmother's determination to keep Kristen in Brookside Falls, and a family secret that is revealed on Christmas Eve. Will the deceit that threatens to break them apart change their lives forever? What will Christmas bring them?

# Granting Her Wish

Emma Kaye

Danielle Thiessen has nothing when she's tossed back in time to the 1960s, not even her memory. Nothing seems right, except how she feels in the arms of the handsome soldier who comes to her rescue.

Vietnam veteran Lee Russell is struggling to return to civilian life in a society that reviles him for serving his country. He no longer feels at home, except when holding Danielle in his arms.

She doesn't belong in his time and he doesn't belong back home. Could they belong to each other?

Dedicated to ~

My husband. Always.

Our wonderful kids. Mommy loves you.

My fellow Scribes. This has been an incredible experience. May it be the first of many.

Our wonderful editor, Mallory Braus, for all your hard work on making sure our stories shine.

# Granting Her Wish
## by Emma Kaye

Danielle Thiessen smiled like an idiot as she held open the door of the café. The place had been like a second home to her the past few weeks. Riding the PATH train back and forth to Manhattan for countless job interviews during the day while tending bar each night, she'd needed all the caffeine she could get.

She breathed in the delicious aroma of freshly brewed coffee and cinnamon rolls that wafted out the door along with a blast of warm air. The frigid wind of December in Hoboken made quick work of the warmth, but the cold couldn't touch her today.

An elderly man in a fedora and thick, horn-rimmed glasses shuffled through the open door. He tipped his hat in thanks and her grin widened. He probably thought she was a lunatic, but she didn't care. Nothing could bring her down. She undid the buttons on her knee-length, cherry-red wool coat.

She struggled with the zipper underneath while she waited in line, only managing to yank it free when she arrived at the front.

"Merry Christmas, Wendy. Small coffee, please."

"Merry Christmas! How's the job search going, sweetie?" Wendy plucked a festive red-and-green paper cup from the stack and filled it with the strong Colombian brew she knew Dani preferred.

"Great." Dani beamed. "I'm just coming back from my final interview. I got the job! I start right after New Year's."

Wendy stretched across the counter to give Dani a quick hug. "That's wonderful news." She pulled back and picked up a plate of sugar cookies decorated like ornaments. "How about a little treat to celebrate?"

Dani shook her head. "No, thanks. Coffee's fine." Treats would have to wait until her first paycheck. Her bank account was running on fumes. She'd have skipped the drink altogether if they would've allowed her to sit there without ordering something. Wendy wouldn't mind, but her boss? Uh, no.

She passed her money to Wendy and dropped the change into the tip jar. It wasn't much, but Wendy needed the help. Dani wasn't the only one with shaky finances. She and Wendy worked nights together at the bar and often shared tips on how to make their meager incomes stretch as far as possible. Wendy knew just how much it pained Dani to be in debt.

Just a few weeks to get through before she could rest easy. She'd scraped enough together to pay January's rent since that would be due before her first paycheck hit her account. Utilities would be late, but she'd worked out a payment plan with the utility company and she'd be only a few days behind.

A knot formed in her stomach just thinking about it. What choice did she have? Thank God those days were almost behind her.

Dani draped her purse over the back of a chair before pulling out her little notebook to jot down some figures. She stifled a groan as she sat, her feet aching from her pretty, but not exactly sensible, boots. She wasn't looking forward to the walk home.

All she needed was a little break. A few moments to think things through. She wrote down the salary she'd been promised so she could figure out what her checks would look like.

The credit cards would take a while. They'd gotten out of hand once her mom's medical bills started streaming in. But if she maintained her current spartan lifestyle a few extra months, she'd get a handle on it before too long.

She scrutinized her calculations and swore under her breath. She'd forgotten all about taxes. She reworked her numbers. The new figures made her stomach plummet.

Her head dropped into her hands. She was so screwed. At this rate, she wouldn't be out of debt until her forties. She shivered from the cold seeping through the glass window at her side.

"Everything okay?"

She swiveled in her chair to locate the source of the voice and found herself face-to-face with the old man in the fedora. She hadn't realized they sat so close.

"Sure, I'm fine," she lied.

His eyes narrowed and lips pursed in a thoughtful expression. He wasn't buying it. "I understand. But, you know, sometimes it's easier to tell your problems to a stranger."

"Yeah, I suppose." She grimaced. "Of course, it's not like I have any friends to talk to anyway. I'm new in town."

"I've been married almost fifty years. My wife tells me I'm a good listener."

"Fifty years? Wow. The longest relationship I've had was a year."

His lips quivered but he just watched her, a patient expression on his face, his head tilted slightly to one side.

The urge to spill all her secrets bubbled up. Her eyes burned with the heat of unshed tears.

She sniffed and dabbed at her nose with a crumpled napkin. The rough paper scratched her upper lip. She'd given her last tissue to a mother with a crying toddler on the train.

"I was going to have such a great life, you know? Get a great job. Make lots of money. The works. Completely independent, with no one to worry about but myself. Exactly what I wanted." The lights in her home would go on when she flipped the switch. No worries. Not like when she was a kid. "So, I packed up my stuff and moved here from South Jersey. I had it all planned out. New York City was the place to be. So many opportunities. I made sure I saved enough money to tide me over while I landed the perfect job."

"I take it you haven't had any luck finding that job?"

She threw her crumpled napkin on the table.

"Nope. Got it. I start in a few weeks. Great base pay plus commission when I pass a certain level of sales."

The wrinkles in his forehead deepened as he tilted his head to consider her. "Then why the sad face?"

"It's not enough. Right after I moved, I found out my mom has lung cancer."

He patted her shoulder. "I'm sorry." He'd rolled up his sleeves to the elbows despite the chill in the air, revealing the faded blue tattoo lines of an eagle clutching an American flag on his forearm.

She tucked her shaking hands under her thighs and hunched forward. "Thanks." She shrugged. "She didn't even call me. I found out when she ran out of money and couldn't stand the only places she could afford. She moved in and now I'm paying for a part-time caregiver and sleeping on my lumpy sofa. It's all piling up and in the end, I'm going to be left with a heap of unresolved mommy issues, not enough time to come to terms with her, and a whole stack of bills I won't be able to climb out from under for the next twenty years." She twisted her head until her neck gave a satisfying crack. It didn't do much to ease the tension in her shoulders. "I swore to myself I'd never live like this again, yet here I am."

"Sounds like you could use a little luck."

She snorted. "No kidding. But I don't believe in luck. At least, not today."

He smiled. "Understandable. I was young once. Didn't believe in luck much myself, though it has served me well through my many years." He winked. "Even let me keep most of my hair, though my grandpa was balder than a cue ball." He tossed his hat onto the table while patting his full head of silver-gray hair.

She laughed. *Sweet of him to try to cheer me up.*

"I've even shared my luck with others upon occasion." He settled back in his chair.

Dani stifled a sigh. She sensed a story coming on. Her grandmother had been full of them and they all started with the settling back in a chair to get comfy. They usually ended with Dani asleep in her bed. Well, at least she had an excuse not to return home right away. It would be rude to cut him off.

"I was a soldier. Though not by choice. Dodging the draft didn't seem right, so when my number came up, I reported for duty."

Judging by his choice of words and a quick calculation in her head, she guessed, "Vietnam?"

He sighed. "It was a horrible time. I'm an artist. A sensitive soul, my mother used to say. My father figured the army would toughen me up. He wasn't wrong." He fell silent, his gaze fixed somewhere beyond the window.

She picked at her cup. Did she want to hear the rest of his story? He'd drawn her in, despite herself, but…

"My tour was finally over. One last mission. It went wrong, of course. Last missions always seemed to go wrong."

"I'm sorry," she whispered.

His eyes glinted with unshed tears. He patted her hand, the feel of his skin warm and paper-thin against her fingers.

"I was there for a reason and luck saw me through." He paused. His eyes glazed over as if he no longer saw the café around him. "We were passing through a little hamlet when Charlie attacked. The villagers scattered, but this little girl just froze. Right in the middle of everything.

"I grabbed her, but we were pinned down. I couldn't move for fear she'd get hit. I could feel the thud of the bullets all around us. See the little puffs of dirt fly up as the bullets struck.

"My luck saw me through. Or hers did. I don't know. But we didn't get a scratch. It ended in short order, though it seemed like forever before I handed that child back to her family.

"Her grandma was a witch, I suppose. Grabbed my hand and started mumbling. I couldn't understand a word. She picked up one of my bullet casings, a handful of dirt, and shattered glass. She slashed her hand and squeezed blood onto the whole mess, muttering all the while and refusing to release me. When she finished, she filled a little canvas bag and passed it to me. Her daughter told me it was a bag of luck. That it would one day grant me what I needed most."

Dani pressed a hand to her chest and leaned forward. "And did it?"

He shrugged. "I met my wife before I had the chance to use it. I never needed anything else once I had her." He scanned the room, stopping at a spot somewhere behind her. A small smile lit his face.

"That's lovely." Fifty years and still so deeply in love he couldn't talk about his wife without smiling.

He dragged a fabric shopping bag across his table, rooted around, and pulled out a small, black velvet bag. He held it in the palm of his hand. "I melted the casing, mixed in the rest and made it into this ornament. Perhaps it has some magic remaining?" He held it out to her. "Why don't you give it a try?"

She waved him off. "Oh, no. I couldn't." She really couldn't. Knowing what was in it turned her stomach. She did not want to touch that thing.

He slipped the ties open and tilted the bag. The meager sunlight streaming in through the heavily fogged window seemed to brighten and splashed off a delicate, heart-shaped ornament.

She gasped in delight. It was stunning. Intricate silver filigree worked through a beautiful mosaic of red-and-green stained glass. She extended a tentative finger toward it but pulled back. "It's gorgeous."

He nudged it toward her. "It's Christmas. Anything is possible at Christmas. Besides, what could it hurt?"

She shrugged. "Well, I suppose a little extra money could come in handy." She reached out, at the same time noticing the inscription. *Always.* Wouldn't that be nice.

Her fingers traced the delicate lines of the ornament. Her heart sped up with longing. Moisture flooded her mouth and she swallowed. Her vision blurred. She blinked. Red and gold blended and swirled before her eyes until the swaying colors filled her sight.

"Are you okay, little lady?"

She stumbled to her feet, the old man's voice an echo in her ears. "Um, yeah. I just…need a little air." She staggered to the door, fingers pressed to her pounding temples. She fell out onto the frozen asphalt.

ꕥ

"You okay?"

She stared at the gloved hand before her. "What…what happened?" The pavement dug into her hands and knees. *Why am I on the ground?*

The hand moved closer and she tried to focus. Once the dark leather glove stopped wavering in her vision, she worked her gaze up a khaki green arm, past what she thought must be an insignia of rank, across a wide chest, and all the way to his head.

The soldier's face swam before her eyes for a second before settling enough to get a good look. A fair complexion, bright green eyes, and a gently turned-down mouth were topped by closely cropped dark blond hair. But something was odd about his uniform. She couldn't place it.

"Do I know you?" she asked, her voice pitched higher and faster than normal.

He shook his head. "No, ma'am. I was walking by when you came flying straight into my path. Wish I'd seen you sooner. I could have caught you."

"Ma'am?"

He grinned. "Would you prefer Miss?"

"I'm certainly not a ma'am. I'm only…" She frowned. *Why can't I remember how old I am?* She swallowed the bitter taste of bile and forced herself to breathe.

A featherlight touch swept across her brow, brushing her hair back from her forehead. "Looks like you took a bit of a bump to the head."

Her arms trembled as she pushed herself back. With one shaking hand, she prodded a knot on her forehead and winced. With her other hand, she clasped the open palm he held out to her. His gloves were cool to the touch. Where were her gloves? The wind shoved her jacket wide open.

She stumbled to her feet, grateful for the steady, strong presence of the man beside her. A car horn beeped. The tone grated on her nerves. It sounded wrong. A classic car passing by slammed on its brakes, tires squealing, almost ramming into another old-fashioned car in front of it.

Her thoughts whirled. She flexed her legs trying to ease the ache in her knees. Why had she been on the ground? Nothing made sense.

"I'm Leland Russell." He squeezed her hand lightly before letting go. "Call me Lee."

She pulled her coat closed, fumbling with the zipper. The darn thing refused to come together until he brushed her hands aside and quickly zipped her up.

"Thanks."

"And you are?" He raised an eyebrow and peered at her face.

"I'm—" She cut herself off to rack her brain. "I—I don't know." Panic squeezed her heart. "Why don't I know my name?" Her head ached. A sharp pain stabbed at her behind the eyes. She rubbed them until she saw spots. *What's wrong with me?* "What's going on?" Her voice rose to hysterical levels.

Lee grabbed her by the shoulders. She tried to shake him off, but he didn't let go. "Calm down. It's okay." She batted at his hands, pushed at his chest, but he didn't move. He pulled her to him, repeating the same two phrases over and over.

Gradually her trembling eased. Her

breathing evened out. He was right. She needed to calm down. Panicking didn't help anything.

He tilted her chin, forcing her to peer into his eyes. "You must have hit your head harder than I thought. Let's get you to a hospital, have a doctor check you out. I'm sure it will all come back to you in no time."

Gorgeous green eyes, flecked with gold and rimmed with thick, long lashes. Lashes that were closer to black than the dark blond of his hair. Speechless, she nodded, but regretted it when the movement jarred her head, sending more shooting pains across her forehead. "Okay. Just give me a moment. I'm not sure I can walk."

"Lean against me. Let me know when you feel a little steadier."

He wrapped an arm around her shoulder and molded her to his side. Muscles flexed against the arm she wrapped around his waist to hold herself up. A faint hint of bleach and starch mixed with the spicy smell of his aftershave. The strangely familiar, relaxing scent eased her headache. His body deflected some of the freezing wind and warmth surged through her.

"I don't see a purse." He looked her up and down while she snuggled against him. "Maybe check your pockets, see if you have something with your name on it?"

"Okay." A search of her pockets came up empty except for a set of keys. She dangled them off her finger for his inspection. "This is all." She dropped them into his open palm.

He held them up and squinted at the key chain. "It's faded, but I can make out D-A-N-I." He passed the keys back to her. "Dani. Sound familiar?

Maybe the beginning of Danielle?"

"Danielle." She closed her eyes and rolled the name around in her head. *Danielle. No. Not quite.* "Dani?" *Yes, that feels right.* "Yes. I think so."

"See, we've solved one riddle already." He smiled down at her. "You up for a little walk yet, Dani?"

"Yes. Let's go." She would have stumbled along on her own, but he kept a firm arm around her. He weaved them in and out among rowdy dockworkers carrying old-fashioned metal lunch pails. He stopped frequently to let her rest, often risking the curses of passersby forced to skirt around them.

She could smell the water, but couldn't catch a glimpse, tucked against his side as she was. She would have liked to walk along the water's edge, but didn't object when he turned away from the docks to head up a side street. She nestled closer to his strong form instead.

Finally, they arrived at the emergency entrance of St. Mary's Hospital. She greeted the warmth of the reception area with relief. While Lee explained the situation to the nurse on duty, Dani shifted from foot to foot in a failed attempt to relieve the pressure on her aching toes.

She tried not to stare at the nurse's white hat and skirt. On an older woman, she might have understood the old-fashioned outfit, but this nurse couldn't have been more than thirty. Where were the scrubs and sneakers?

A harsh jangling noise caught her attention and she stared at the ancient phone at the reception desk in confusion. *What the hell?*

A young, pretty, blonde nurse came around the corner. "Lee!" She wrapped her arms around him and kicked up her feet. He lifted her off the ground in a huge bear hug. The nurse's laugh caused an unexpected pang of jealousy. *Don't be ridiculous.*

"Dani?"

She jerked her attention away from her irrational emotions. "What? I'm sorry. Did you ask me something?"

"Tracy asked if you want me to stay with you." Lee leaned against the nurse's desk, one ankle crossed over the other. When Tracy tried to link her arm through his, he shook her off. Dani repressed her smirk. "Or would you rather I left?"

Panic welled. He couldn't leave. She'd be all alone. She gripped his hand. "Stay, please. I don't want to be left alone." Her heart beat faster and her gaze skittered around the crowded waiting area. Everyone and everything seemed so strange. She shivered as a young woman dressed like a hippie in a long skirt, tie-dyed shirt, and fringed jacket gave them the evil eye.

He pushed upright, then led her to some chairs a few feet past the sinister hippie.

"Baby killer," she mumbled under her breath.

Lee tensed but Dani stopped dead.

She clenched her fists, resisting the urge to strike out. "How dare you?" She stomped over to the girl, who cowered back where she sat cross-legged on her seat. "He's a soldier. He deserves your respect."

Lee tugged on her arm. "It's okay. Let's go."

She gave the girl one last scowl. Hippie chick ducked her head, letting her long hair fall across her flushed face.

Lee hadn't moved, but stepped back when she turned. His shoulders hunched forward, his hands shoved deep into his pockets. He didn't look at her, but seemed focused on a point somewhere above her head.

The expression on his face almost made her cry. She'd expected anger. All she saw was acceptance.

ꟾ

The bulb above Dani's head flickered. The flashes of shadow and light were sure to drive her mad. She needed a distraction.

She slouched forward in the waiting room chair and tried to inspect Lee without drawing attention to the fact. Elbows propped on her knees, head in her hands, she peeked at him through her lashes. Keeping her eyes at half-mast had the added benefit of easing her headache.

As a distraction, he rated pretty high. He paced between her chair and the station where the pretty blonde latched on to him whenever he came her way. Dani tamped down the green-eyed monster. She had no right to be jealous. He was a nice man, a soldier, who stopped to help a woman in trouble. That didn't make him hers.

Not that she'd mind. His uniform hugged his butt and accentuated a physique born from long days of physical labor. Or so she imagined. She really had no idea. He hadn't said more than a few words to her since they arrived.

He saved his conversation for Tracy, who kept her voice low and grabbed him whenever his pacing brought him within reach. She only released him when her duties called her away.

Tracy left to assist a patient so he swung back Dani's way. She dragged her coat off the chair next to her. "Do you want to sit?"

He dropped into the chair with a smile. "Sorry. Is my pacing driving you mad? I've never been one for sitting around."

She smiled back. "I have a feeling I'm not either, but every time I move my head pounds." She flicked a hand toward the nurse. "Does she have any idea when the doctor might see me?" Good. She kept her intense dislike out of her voice.

"Tracy said it won't be much longer." He glanced toward the nurses' station. Dani forced her hands to unclench. "I tried, but she won't move you up in line. Not even for me."

"She your girlfriend?" Dani had already noted the absence of a wedding ring on his finger.

"Sister."

A ridiculous wave of relief washed over her. "Oh. Well, I wouldn't want to get her into trouble." Tracy was such a great nurse, after all. Wouldn't even break the rules for family. Of course Dani should wait her turn. "I'm sure there are more pressing cases." Her headache wasn't even all that bad.

"Yeah, well, I think she just wants to keep me here as long as possible." He shrugged, his smile slipping.

She raised an eyebrow and kept silent, hoping he'd elaborate. She'd learned the silence trick well. People couldn't seem to resist filling in the blanks in a conversation, often divulging much more than they might normally.

Okay. Why did she know that? The memory slipped away, gathering like fog on the edge of her vision. Nothing solid enough to grab.

He leaned back and rubbed at his temples. His wide shoulder brushed against her so she shifted to give him room. "I think your headache's contagious," he said with a quick grin. True to her expectations, he continued when she didn't reply. "I hadn't meant for anyone in my family to see me in my uniform."

Did that make some kind of sense? "Why?"

He shrugged. "Not sure what you know about it, but we were instructed to change out of our uniforms the second we got back to the States. It's not a good idea to wear them at home nowadays."

She frowned. "I don't understand."

"You must have blocked out the news along with everything else." He leaned forward and dropped his head in his hands, but twisted sideways to stare back at her. "That woman back there…"

"What about her?" The hippie woman in question had left shortly after Dani confronted her. Dani hadn't been able to overhear, but the woman had approached the nurses' station, had a heated argument with Tracy, then left in a huff.

"That kind of attitude's getting more and more common. We're not exactly welcomed home with open arms when we finish our tours."

The story sounded familiar but remote. As if it were something she'd read about, but not experienced. "I don't understand. She's crazy. Stoned, too, I'd guess from the smell. Most people would be grateful for the sacrifices soldiers make to protect our country."

"You must have family in the military. Maybe a husband?"

She jerked. Crap. She hadn't even thought about that. "Oh my God. What if I have a husband somewhere?" She took a deep breath, squeezed her eyes shut. Her left hand trembled. She held it up, but couldn't look. Could she have forgotten someone so important? Someone she must love dearly to have committed her life to him?

Warmth engulfed her hand. Her eyes flew open. Lee massaged the knuckles of her bare ring finger. He brought her hand close to his face, then shook his head. "Nope. No ring. No mark. I'd say you're single."

Her breath left her in a *whoosh.* She stared at their joined hands. He continued his massage up to her palm. She stifled a groan. Damn, that felt good. Her muscles relaxed and tension of another sort built. Heat flamed across her cheeks. She let out a nervous little cough.

He let her hand drop back in her lap, then rubbed his hands up and down his legs as if drying them.

"So, um, you were saying about taking off your uniform?" The heat flared all over her body this time. Her mind inserted the images to go along with her words. "Oh! I didn't mean—I meant—"

Damn. Now he was blushing. She'd never made a man blush before. At least, she didn't think so. She dropped her gaze to the floor but peeked at him through the corner of her eye.

He cleared his throat. "I—uh—" He rubbed the back of his neck and gave a short laugh. "Uniform. I wore my uniform because I planned on going back."

"Back where? Afghanistan? Iraq?"

His brows scrunched together and his mouth gaped open. "That bump on the head must have addled your memory more than we thought." He shook his head. "Vietnam."

"I don't understand. I didn't think we had any bases there." She tilted her head to get a better view of his face. "We pulled out of there, like, forty-something years ago. I didn't think we'd gone back."

Why was he gaping at her like she'd gone nuts?

ꟷ

"Dani?" Tracy stood next to Dani's chair. She clasped a clipboard to her chest and dipped her head toward a set of doors. "Can you please follow me?"

Lee continued to stare at her as she gathered up her coat. *What had she said?* Her keys fell out of her pocket with a clatter. He picked them up and the moment passed. His fingers lingered against hers when he gave them back. Her hand tingled from the contact.

Tracy drummed her fingers against her clipboard, so Dani shoved the keys back in her pocket as she followed Tracy down a long hallway.

"We'll run a few tests," she said over her shoulder. "Then I'll get you a room to wait for the doctor."

Before long, Tracy walked her down yet another hall to a small room with a curtain-enclosed area to await the doctor. Dani perched on the edge of the bed. The stiff mattress crinkled when she moved. Tracy said a few words to a man mopping the linoleum floor just outside her small space before arranging the privacy curtains. The cloying stench of cigarette smoke mixed with the antiseptic stink of the cleaner, making Dani's nose itch. She shoved back on the bed to get a little distance.

The edge of the bed tilted. Dani looked up in surprise to see Tracy settling in at the foot. She leaned against the metal footboard and smiled. Dani raised her brows in question. What could Lee's sister possibly want?

"I want to thank you for bringing Lee in here." Her voice trembled and she stared at a spot near Dani's left shoulder.

"You're welcome?" This was the most confusing day.

Tracy chuckled and met Dani's gaze. "I'm sorry you were hurt. I know it wasn't some well-laid plan to get Lee's attention. But it did. And I'm glad." She shrugged. "I just wanted you to know that whatever else happens—if you need anything—just let me know. I owe you."

"Oh. Well. Thank you. That's very nice." Dani rubbed at a small scratch on her knuckle. She tilted her head and regarded Lee's sister. "I'm still not sure I understand. Lee thought you'd be upset at seeing him in his uniform. But, you've seemed nothing but happy anytime you're near him."

Tracy patted Dani's hand. "Lee just got home and we're all having a hard time adjusting. He left a note this morning saying he meant to reenlist." Tears clouded her eyes. "I don't think he planned on coming home. Ever."

Dani scooted over and wrapped her arms around the crying woman. "Shh. I know it's tough having your brother overseas, but you could see him when he comes home on leave and talk to him on the Web." *What in the world have I stepped into?*

"Web? What?" Tracy shook her head. "No. I don't think he planned on taking leave. I don't think he planned on surviving long enough."

Dani's mouth dropped open and she pulled back. "You're kidding! Why?"

A doctor burst through the curtain. A cigarette hung from his lips. He plucked it out and blew a long stream of noxious smoke toward the ceiling.

Tracy jumped up. She wiped discreetly at her eyes as she straightened the bed where she'd been sitting, before standing quietly alongside.

Dani stared at the doctor. How many shocks could she take in one day? "You can't smoke that in here." She couldn't understand the odd expression on his face. His mouth hung open and his eyebrows rose nearly to his receding hairline. "Can you?" she asked, suddenly unsure.

"I can," he replied. He snapped his mouth shut into a strained smile. "Does it bother you?"

Dani bobbed her head.

"Well then, young lady…" He stubbed out the cigarette in an ashtray conveniently placed on a small table on the side of the bed and gave her a more natural grin. "I'll just put this out."

Dani held her breath as he leaned over her for the normal checkup routine. Thankfully, Tracy helped, giving the doctor a chance to stand back and ask questions—from a little distance. At least far enough away that Dani could control her gag reflex. She couldn't remember the last time she'd been so near a smoker who hadn't had to extinguish their cigarette outside a building.

Of course, she couldn't remember a lot of things. That's why she was there.

"I see nothing wrong with you, physically. The bump on your head isn't serious enough to cause memory loss of this type."

She touched the goose-egg lump on her scalp. "Then why can't I remember who I am?" Pain stabbed through her head. She forced herself to breathe. In, out. In, out.

The doctor shrugged. "I can't say for certain. I can only surmise that you experienced some type of emotional trauma that has caused you to block out your memory. Your subconscious went overboard and got rid of much more."

"So, I may not want my memory back? What could have happened?"

"I wish I could help you." He placed a hand on her shoulder. "I've contacted the police. Perhaps they can figure out who you are and what happened. And your memory may come back to you at any time."

Dani nodded, but his words barely registered. What could have happened that was so bad she'd rather forget her whole life rather than remember?

The doctor left, taking Tracy with him. Dani sank onto the bed. She couldn't seem to find a control to raise the back, so she plumped up the pillow as much as it would go and leaned against the vertical posts of the headboard. Like prison bars.

She shivered. *Where had that thought come from?* It must have been the mention of the police. Would they have the answers she sought?

A whisper of sound brought her attention to

the curtain. Lee stuck his head in. "Okay if I come in?"

"Yes, please." Her heart fluttered. "I'm surprised you're still here. You didn't have to stay."

He flashed her a brief smile and stood just within the curtain. If she leaned forward in the small space she could have touched the tight set of his shoulders. He shifted his weight from foot to foot. "I wanted to make sure you were all right. Plus, Tracy thought you might like some company. Was the doctor any help?"

She shook her head. "Not really. He can't find anything wrong with me."

He stepped forward. "That's great. Does he know when you'll get your memory back?"

His leg came to within an inch of her hand. Her fingers ached with the desire to touch him. This was *so* not the time to hit on the man. "He has no idea. Apparently it's a mental problem, not a physical one." Yeah, she was crazy. If he wasn't turned on by her fainting damsel in distress routine, he was sure to love the insane weirdo act.

Lee covered her hand, the edges of his fingers brushing against her thigh where her hand rested in her lap. "Maybe the police will be able to figure it out. They can see if anyone's reported you missing. Or, if someone witnessed what happened to you, we can get this all cleared up."

Her lips trembled in a vain attempt at a reassuring smile. "I'm sure it will all work out." God, did she always lie so much?

*Bam!*

She whipped her head around to see what caused the commotion, but was knocked off the bed and flattened against the floor before she could reach the curtain to pull it aside. A heavy weight settled on her, making it hard to breathe. A loud thumping beat fast as a drum in her ear.

She twisted to the side. Lee lay on top of her, hunched over, covering her body. His chest pressed down on top of her head, his head tucked under, nearly touching the floor. His pulse beat erratically. Sweat drenched his once-crisp shirt.

"Lee?" she whispered, afraid to startle him any further.

Even so, he jerked. His gaze darted left, then right. He untangled himself then sat on his haunches, giving her enough room to move. She shoved off the floor and tried to catch his eye but he hung his head. His shoulders sagged as he rose, holding out a hand to help her up.

"Sorry," he mumbled.

She squeezed his hand. Damn. The poor man must have been through hell.

The second he had her situated back on the bed, he dropped her hand like a hot frying pan. He turned to go, but she lunged forward to grab his arm, refusing to release him when he tried to shrug her off. He'd been so good to her. She couldn't let him leave like this.

"I should go."

"No." He seemed ready to run, so she did the only thing she could think of. "Please, Lee? I'm scared to be alone." Ah, the pity card. It wasn't pretty, but it sure packed a punch.

His arm muscles clenched under her hand. He stood, stiff as a board, with his back to her, one hand holding the curtain open. She peeked past his shoulder and saw a nurse picking up a tray. Apparently the source of the loud noise. Dani held her breath waiting for Lee's response.

The curtain dropped, blocking her view. She turned her attention to the back of his head. A sharp nod told her the shameless plea had worked and she could breathe once more.

But what could she say? She wasn't a therapist. At least, she didn't think so.

"Thank you." She let go of his arm and clenched her hands in her lap. "Has this happened before?"

Another nod.

"Have you talked to anyone about it?"

"No." He rubbed the back of his neck. When he turned to face her, he kept his gaze on the floor. "What's there to say? I hear a loud noise and I dive for cover. Why would anyone want to listen to a coward?"

"Oh, Lee." Tears choked her voice. She had to clear her throat twice before she could continue. "You're not a coward."

His eyes were suspiciously bright as he raised his gaze to hers. "I am. You saw."

She chuckled. "I didn't see much of anything, actually." She grabbed his hand before he could bolt. "Do you want to know why?" Before he had a chance to shake his head, she continued, "Because you threw me to the ground and covered me with your body. Would a coward do that? You didn't run. Or try to save yourself."

"I'm an idiot. Save myself? From what?" he asked in a tone riddled with self-loathing. He swiped his arm across his forehead, mopping up the sweat that glistened on his brow. "A tray of pudding? Yeah. I'm real brave. Just don't throw any dessert my way."

"I don't know much about post-traumatic stress, but I've heard that noise is a trigger. In that moment, it wasn't a tray you heard, it was a bomb or bullets or something deadly like that. And your first thought wasn't to run or to hide. It was to save me." She tapped herself on the chest. "A woman you just met who you've spent the day with cooped up in a hospital trying to help. I don't think you're a coward. I think you're a hero."

She wasn't sure how much she helped, but thought his expression lightened ever so slightly. At the very least, he was looking her in the eye again.

ꟹ

Little by little, Lee responded to her halting attempts to lighten the mood. Pretty soon, he regaled her with stories of his childhood. His laughter stopped being so forced. He seemed to make it his mission to entertain her while they waited for the police.

Dani was careful not to wince at the new bruises he'd given her when he'd tossed her to the ground.

The time passed swiftly, but she was getting tired. She wished she could leave the hospital even though she had no place to go.

When two officers entered her room, Lee jumped to attention. He didn't salute, but his posture indicated he had to restrain himself.

Dani crossed her arms over her stomach and straightened on the uncomfortable bed. She had to be careful how she sat. She'd swear a spring was determined to make it up her butt.

Thank goodness the doctor hadn't seen any

reason to admit her. He'd let her stay here only so she could have some semblance of privacy for her interview with the police.

"Hello, Miss. I'm Officer O'Malley. This is Officer Hanlon." Officer O'Malley had short, slicked-back dark hair and a thick mustache that quivered when he spoke. He flashed his badge, then pulled out a small black notebook and pen. Officer Hanlon looked to be about ten or fifteen years younger than his partner. He stood silently with his arms crossed and alternated staring at her with picking at a pimple on the side of his neck.

After half an hour, O'Malley flipped his notebook closed. "We'll see what we can find, Miss." He handed her a card. "Call the station if you remember anything useful." His tone indicated he wasn't expecting a call anytime soon. He motioned for Lee to follow him.

She dropped the card in her lap and plucked at the starched sheet as she waited for Lee's return. The minutes dragged by. What was taking them so long? She stood and eased over to the slit in the curtain. Murmuring male voices filtered into her room from a few feet away. She slipped one finger along the edge of the curtain to nudge it an inch to the side so she could peek through. Hopefully without being noticed.

Officer O'Malley stood with his back to her facing Lee, who ran his hand through his buzz cut as he listened. He gazed past the cop, directly at her. She froze. Damn, caught in the act.

Wait, was that a wink? But Lee had already turned his attention away from her. Within minutes he shook the officer's hand. They parted and Dani hopped back onto the bed. She hadn't stopped bouncing before Lee stood grinning at her side. Heat washed across her face as she cast about for a way to bring the attention off her unsuccessful stint as a spy.

"So. What did O'Malley have to say?" She sounded huffy. Justifiably, she thought. Why the hell was the officer discussing her with a stranger? Not that she would have kept anything from Lee at this point. But, really. What right did the officer have to make that decision for her?

His grin widened. "Officer O'Malley is one suspicious police officer. He's looking for his big break and he's determined to find it. Down with the commies." He gave a little fist-bump in the air.

She cocked her head. "What?"

"I can tell you he does not share the general attitude about Vietnam. He spent fifteen minutes complaining that he was too old for the draft and couldn't go over there to kick some commie butt." His grin faded. "He wanted me to tell him all about it."

"What did you say?" She kept her voice low and soothing. Had he been diagnosed with PTSD, or did he have no idea why he suffered?

She could smack that officer for being such an insensitive jerk.

Lee's hands clenched so tightly his knuckles whitened. O'Malley should count himself lucky Lee hadn't taken a swing at him.

"I told him he didn't want to know." He shook himself and lost the faraway look as he gazed into her eyes.

The urge to wipe her mouth and make sure she hadn't drooled was strong enough to make her fingers twitch. Damn, the man had beautiful eyes.

Such a clear green, with golden specks that made her think of a tree she used to sit under when she was a child. She would climb up into its boughs to hide when she needed time away from home. In the fall, bright yellow leaves would intersperse with the green. She'd spend hours reading—

Her eyes widened. "I just remembered something from when I was little!"

He beamed and sat on the bed next to her. "Wonderful. See? It'll all come back to you. We just need to give it some time."

She shivered when the warmth of his thigh brushed against her leg, her breath lodged in her throat. She gulped and stared down at his leg so close to hers. She let her hair fall forward to hide the blush that surely turned her cheeks as red as her car.

She gasped. "I had a red car. It was a piece of crap, but I loved it. I just sold it." Her brows knitted in thought. "Why did I sell it?" The headache that more or less hovered at the back of her skull reminded her of its presence. She rubbed at her temples.

Lee wrapped an arm around her shoulders. "Don't push too hard. Give it time."

She leaned into his comforting embrace. "I don't have time," she mumbled.

His body tensed and she jerked her attention back up to his face.

"What do you mean?" he asked.

She got the distinct impression he didn't like what she'd said. "I don't have time. Where am I going to go? The doctor says there's nothing wrong with me. They're not going to let me stay here." She grabbed her coat from the side of the bed. A search of the pockets was fruitless, but she'd known it would be. She'd checked them at least a dozen times already. The only things she had were a meager set of keys with a faded key chain. She held them up. "These are all I have." She ran her finger along the edge of the key that appeared most like a house key. The ridges scratched her skin, but gave no clue to what she should do. "I have no idea what this unlocks. Where am I supposed to go while I wait for my memory to return?"

He stared at her for a moment, then took a deep breath. He let it out slowly and rubbed his palms down his thighs. "You can stay with me."

Speechless. She opened and closed her mouth but nothing, not a word, came out. Stay with him? A thrill shot up her spine. Good thing she'd left her suit jacket on so he couldn't see the way her nipples tightened at the thought of going home with him.

He laughed and pushed her chin up. "I take it you weren't gunning for an invitation?"

She shook her head.

"That's good. Because Officer O'Malley seems to think that's what you were after."

"Wait. What?"

"I mentioned he was a suspicious man. Since he hasn't heard of any missing women and the doctor gave you a clean bill of health, the officer seems to think you're trying to take advantage of me." He leaned close. She forgot to breathe. "Are you trying to take advantage of me?"

His eyes had a distinct twinkle and she gave a shaky laugh. Oh, yeah. "'Course not." Not exactly ringing with indignation, but she was lucky it hadn't come out like she'd been sucking on a helium tank.

He grinned and gave her the once-over. "Not that I would mind if you were."

*Oh, my.*

ཀྵ

Dani huddled inside her jacket and tried to control her violent shivering as she followed Lee through the streets of Hoboken. Her bright red wool coat looked nice, but it did nothing to keep out the icy wind and snow that insisted on blowing down her neck. Her hair plastered against her cheek. She had to concentrate to avoid stepping in the snow piled up along the edges of the sidewalks or slipping on the ice hidden beneath the newly fallen snow.

Her high-heeled boots clicked along, scrunching her freezing toes together. She wanted nothing more than to toss them aside and bury her feet in a thick down comforter. She slipped, but Lee steadied her with a hand at her elbow. She wouldn't say no to sharing that blanket.

Damn, she hoped she didn't have a boyfriend. If she did, her relationship was in serious trouble because she didn't think she'd be able to forget Lee as easily as she'd forgotten her past.

And she wasn't sure she wanted to forget him. She couldn't shake the feeling that she'd never been so well taken care of by anyone. His hand still had a firm grip on her elbow, guiding her along the path and keeping her steady.

His boots were much more practical than hers. He hadn't slipped once.

*What am I doing?* She needed to walk on her own. Why was it so easy to put all her troubles and cares in the hands of this stranger? She never trusted anyone like this. She never let men hold the door for her, and hated it when they put their hands on her as if she were too delicate to walk on her own.

Why could she remember that, when other things, like her last name and whether she had a family that missed her, were completely gone?

"Here we are."

His strained voice broke through her thoughts. His gaze locked on the cheerful house before them.

He'd stopped in front of a redbrick house with a white awning framed by large, multicolored Christmas bulbs. A huge wreath covered half the door. A thin dusting of snow coated the three steps and a black umbrella leaned against the wall next to the bright blue door.

A light clicked on. Tracy propped her hip against the storm door to hold it open, beaming at Dani like she were a beloved family member. "Don't just stand there! Come on in." She gestured for them to enter. Dani felt the slight pressure of Lee's hand at the small of her back.

The warmth trickling through her eased some of the pressure of the situation. She smiled with a sigh of relief as the heat of the entryway embraced her.

Tracy reached for Lee's jacket as Dani tugged at her zipper with stiff, cold fingers. When she yanked the end free, Lee stepped close to slide the jacket off her shoulders. His body pressed against her backside in the small entry.

She wanted to lean into him but swept aside the temptation. They weren't lovers. She had no right. He was being a gentleman, not trying to cop a feel. Not that she'd have minded.

She avoided his eyes as he handed her jacket to his sister.

"What are you doing here, Trace?" A heavy dose of suspicion laced his words.

"Just picking up some cookies Mom made for the kids and sticking a lasagna in the oven." She winked at Dani. "I won't be here long. I have to get home and make sure the kids get to bed."

"Where are Mom and Dad?" he asked.

Dani surveyed the room, noticing the quiet for the first time. Lee had said living with his parents hadn't been going well. Hence, his presence downtown that morning. From the way he'd described his mother she'd been expecting a much more…exuberant…welcome.

"They're at my place. Dad's helping Rich fix our refrigerator. Good thing it's so cold. All our food's on the porch. Anyway, Mom wanted to make sure you were fed, so she asked that I get your dinner started. She's been cooking up a storm." She patted her stomach. "I swear, I put on ten pounds every time she comes over."

"Why don't we head over with you? I can help Dad and Rich." He slipped his coat back over his shoulders and started doing up the buttons.

Tracy put her hands over his. "No, you two stay here. We're full up over at my place." She shoved the jacket off Lee's shoulders, then turned to Dani. "You don't mind, do you? This snow looks like it might get bad. I don't have enough room for all of us and it might not be safe for you to make your way back here later."

He raised his brows at Tracy. A becoming blush stained her cheeks and she whipped around to grab her jacket off the banister. She shrugged into it, keeping her head tilted away. A knitted hat and gloves followed. Within minutes she'd bustled out with a quick hug for both Dani and her brother.

Dani watched in amusement. Something was up. "So, what was that all about?"

Lee chuckled as he hung his jacket in a small, packed closet by the door. "My sister's playing matchmaker."

She put her coat into his outstretched hand then wrapped her arms around herself. The air still held a hint of cold from outside. She shivered. "Matchmaker?"

"She lives five doors down." He grinned. "I'm pretty sure I could make it that far even in a blizzard." He hung Dani's jacket next to his, then gestured down the hall. "Let's get away from the door. If I'm not mistaken, it will be much warmer in the living room." He showed her through to the next room.

A roaring fire cast its glowing light and heat about the cozy room. She walked right up to it and stuck out her hands to soak in the warmth. Lee did the same. The smell of pine wafted up from the boughs draped over the mantel. A white porcelain Nativity set dominated the center.

"Thought so."

He plucked a crystal wineglass from amidst the Christmas decorations. She swung her head up and saw a matching glass and a bottle of wine—already uncorked. She couldn't help it, she burst out laughing.

She wrapped her arms around herself, bent double, her sides threatening to split. She collapsed onto the couch. Lee lowered himself beside her, his deep chortle felt more than heard.

All the stress of the day flowed away along with the mingled sounds of their laughter. Her stomach ached from laughing so hard. She hiccuped as she turned his way.

Noses bumped. She jerked back with another hiccup. The arm of the sofa kept her from going too far. She couldn't avoid touching him, they crowded together so tightly. She should get up. Move to the fire. Warm her hands. She didn't move. Couldn't.

She stared into his eyes. The hunger there almost scared her with its intensity. Her breath hitched. He would kiss her now. She wanted him to kiss her now.

He didn't move, either. He seemed struck with the same inability to break eye contact. How long did they stay that way? Could have been hours.

She couldn't stand it any longer. She leaned in.

At the exact moment Dani leaned in, Lee drew back. He cleared his throat and rose to retrieve the bottle of wine from the mantel. "We might as well enjoy the wine. Tracy will be upset if it goes to waste."

She stood on shaky legs to grab the wineglass he'd placed on the coffee table when they'd collapsed, insensible with laughter. She ran her finger down the stem and tried to still her racing thoughts.

Did he want her, or not?

She passed him the glass, noticing how carefully he plucked the crystal from her hand so their fingers didn't touch. Or was she making something out of nothing?

Her ankle twisted in her high-heeled boots, so she pulled down the zipper and kicked them off. She groaned. Her eyes closed in bliss as her feet flattened out on the soft shag carpet. “Oh, that feels so good.”

He made a strangled, moaning noise of his own. Her eyes flew open to examine his face. “You okay?”

“Uh-huh.” He relaxed his death grip on the bottle to pour the deep-red wine. After handing her a glass, he took a big gulp from his own.

She took a cautious sip, enjoying the rich, fruity flavor that flowed across her tongue. She didn’t recognize the label. “Your sister’s pulling out all the stops. Nineteen sixty-four? She must think you really need to get laid.” She clapped a hand over her mouth. Had she just said that?

Stunned. That’s the way she’d describe the look on his face. Then the rush of blood. He rocked back on his heels. With one hand buried in his pocket, she’d swear he made a little adjustment down there.

Embarrassed? Yes.

Interested? Maybe.

“I’m sorry. Apparently my sister’s more influenced by the free-love movement than I’d have thought. I’m surprised my parents went along with it.”

“Free love?” She put her glass down and strolled around the room. Shag carpet, old wine, black-and-white photos on the mantel. A chain of popcorn and cranberries looped around and around the tree in the corner. “It’s like a blast from the past around here.” Her gaze fell on a stack of newspapers in a bin beside the sofa. The photo caught her attention. Lyndon Johnson? She picked it up for a closer look.

Lee perched on the edge of the sofa. "Yes, while I've been gone, Tracy has gotten into the whole crusade."

She let the paper sag as she gaped at him. "Really? She doesn't seem the type."

He flinched. "I didn't mean it that way. She's happily married. It's just... My return's been hard on my family. They can't understand. I've spent a lot of time in my workshop, trying to work things out for myself. So I made them a gift. It's supposed to bring good luck. I finished it this morning, which is why I chose today..." He tugged at his collar. "Tracy took it especially hard when I was drafted..."

The paper caught her eye again. A buzzing in her head blocked out the rest of his words.

She sank to the floor, the paper flopping open in her lap. The date leaped out at her as if lit with a flashlight.

*December 20, 1965.*

Lee crouched before her. He tugged on her arm. His lips moved, but she couldn't hear a word he said.

Her life flashed through her brain. She remembered everything. Her new job. Her mom. The old man. The ornament.

Now she knew why everything seemed so strange. Why Lee talked about Vietnam and free love. Why the nurses wore those old-fashioned uniforms and the doctor lit up a cigarette in the middle of a hospital room.

Holy crap. She'd traveled back in time.

Somehow, that ornament had transported her

back to the sixties.

The old man had said it would grant her wish. Her wish? She'd wished for more money, not a time warp.

She closed her eyes, that moment clear in her mind. She'd been stressed about her finances. She'd amassed so much debt taking care of her mom, she'd been freaking out about how to manage. Her new job wasn't going to cut it.

Then the old man made that ridiculous comment about luck. She'd never imagined in the slightest that it might actually work.

So why the blast from the past rather than a winning lottery ticket or something?

The light that glinted off that ornament had been so beautiful. She'd reached out a finger to stroke the delicate filigree. And she'd seen…

The inscription.

That was it. *Always,* it had said. She'd thought of the old man and the wife he still loved. Somehow, her wish had gotten all screwed up.

But time travel? Why would her wish bring her back to this point in time? She wasn't even alive yet. She'd gone back almost fifty years into the past.

Fifty years. Damn.

The old man had said he'd been married almost fifty years. Her wish hadn't brought her back. *His* had. He must have been reminiscing about the good old days and she'd gotten caught up in it.

Something cool and hard pressed against her lips. Lee held a glass to her mouth, his hand at the back of her head encouraging her to take a sip. The cold wash of water passing over her lips and down her chin brought her back to the present.

She sputtered and waved the glass away.

He rested the water on the coffee table and helped her stand with a hand under her elbow. She glanced toward the sofa, but he pulled her close until her cheek rested against his chest.

"Are you okay?" he asked. "You scared the devil out of me."

His chin rested on top of her head. She wrapped her arms around his waist. The scent of bleach and starch had faded, but a spicy hint of aftershave remained. She inhaled deeply to calm her racing pulse. She scrunched his shirt in her fist, released it, and smoothed away the wrinkles she'd caused. He was solid. Real. This wasn't a dream.

What should she tell him? "I'm fine. Just got a little dizzy." Understatement of the year. "You know, I think I could use something a little stronger than wine. Do you have anything?"

He eased her onto the sofa, on the end closest to the fire. The heat warmed her, but she shivered anyway when he let her go.

"Sure. I'll be right back."

Hopefully not too soon. She needed time to think up a suitable lie. And lying had never been her strong suit.

ജ൫

Lee returned a few minutes later with a glass of eggnog in one hand and a black velvet bag in the other. He handed her the cup. "Here, take a sip. Let me know if it needs any more rum."

Dani took a sip then stifled her gasp with a cough. "It's fine," she gasped.

He laughed. “Good.”

“Are you trying to get me drunk?” She smiled to let him know she wasn’t serious.

He leaned close. She resisted moving that last inch forward to place a kiss along his jaw. *Damn, he smells good.*

“That’s for me to know…” he whispered in her ear.

“…and me to find out,” she finished for him.

He didn’t move away, so she turned her head.

Her world had turned upside down. She was still shaky. Unsure. Except about him. If anything made sense in this whole mess, it was him.

Their noses grazed. She tilted her head and brushed his mouth lightly with her own. Just enough to tickle.

She couldn’t help herself. He froze, but she let her lips linger.

Her gamble paid off. That slight touching of lips wasn’t enough for him, apparently. He wrapped an arm around her back, bringing her tight against him. The little bag he held bumped against her butt. His other hand went to the base of her neck and tilted her head back as he took her lips with surprising passion.

Surprising, but welcome. She responded with equal fervor. She’d wanted to do this since he’d first helped her up off that sidewalk and supported her all the way to the hospital. Breathing heavily, she broke off the kiss then rested her head against his chest. “I thought you weren’t interested.”

He quaked with laughter. “Not interested? Are you crazy?”

She stiffened. Crazy. That's what he'd think of her if she told him the truth. Was that better or worse than having him think she'd purposely deceived him?

At least when they were keeping things on a friendship level, she hadn't felt this overwhelming urge to tell him all about herself. She wanted to share herself with him. He was the kind of guy she could open up to.

"Hey." He brushed a hair off her forehead. "What's wrong? You can tell me. I'm a good listener."

She pulled her head back to study him. A good listener. Why did that sound so familiar? He stayed still, a gentle smile on his face. She was missing something. Something big. She ran a hand along his jaw. Felt the slight roughness of his five o'clock shadow. Her hand dropped on top of his wrist.

The cuff of his sleeve pushed back. She shoved back his sleeve, revealing the dark blue edge of a recent tattoo.

He must have realized her intent because he folded his sleeve up to his elbow. "An eagle and the American flag. The guys in my platoon all got it one night." His laugh held an uneasy note. "It wasn't one of my brightest moves." He traced the edges with his finger. "Does it bother you?" he asked in a hesitant voice.

She shook her head. That buzzing had returned. This couldn't be possible. "It was you."

"What?"

"The old man. The ornament. It was you."

Confusion clouded his gaze. He rubbed his chin and grimaced.

"I *feel* old some days. I've seen enough..." He hesitated. "I thought it would be different when I got home. I thought it was over. But the nightmare followed me home. I can never return to who I was before. I'm so tired. Have been, ever since I got back." He put a finger under her chin to capture her gaze. "Not so much since I met you."

Tears burned her eyes, but she couldn't let them fall. He wouldn't understand and she couldn't explain it to him. So she kissed him. Clutched his shirt. Held him hostage. Claimed his lips. Claimed his body. Wanted to claim his soul.

Crazy was right. She'd never gone so overboard for a man. But he was different. She could fall for him. Given some time.

Maybe the ornament hadn't been completely out of whack bringing her here.

They separated after a few minutes. Both of them unsteady and gasping for air.

"I do have an ornament, though. Funny you should mention it." His hands met behind her back and he brought the little bag forward. He left his other arm wrapped around her. In order to open the bag, he had to pull her close against his side, his hands hovering over her lap. Her body tingled and she wished he'd throw the bag across the room so he could put his hands to better use.

Then she registered what he'd said. "An ornament?"

He nodded. The ornament slipped out of its bag into the palm of his hand. "I finished this earlier today. This is the gift I planned to give to Tracy." He inspected it with a frown. "Funny. I thought I'd left this somewhere else, but when I went into the kitchen, there it was."

The lights from the Christmas tree blinked on the stained glass swinging from the silken, cream-colored tassel. The ornament twirled in his fingers. Flashes of red and green reflected off the walls. It was as beautiful as she remembered.

All she needed to do was touch it. Touch it and wish to return home. That's what she wanted, right? To return to her own time? Start her new job, make her mom's last few days comfortable, get on with her own life.

Her hand trembled. She reached toward the red-and-green heart, but hesitated. "You made this?"

"Yes. I brought the materials home with me." He shrugged. "I just wanted something beautiful to come out of my time in Nam. I thought it might bring my family some comfort at Christmas." He attempted a smile. A sheen of unshed tears coated his eyes.

"I think they'd rather have you." Her heart twisted.

"Nah." He swiped a hand across his brow. "I've been a mess since I've been back. They're better off without me."

She traced a line from his ear to the tip of his chin with her finger. "That's not true."

"You heard that woman. You must have seen the protests. And you saw what I did at the hospital. I'm not fit to be here anymore. I've changed. I…" He paused and turned his head into the palm of her hand, his eyes closed. "I have nightmares. I wake up screaming, soaking wet with sweat. I scare them."

She guided his hand toward the coffee table and the ornament slipped from his fingers. She clutched his hands to her chest. They sat there, forehead to forehead, until his eyes opened. She captured his gaze. "Oh, honey. Of course you're having nightmares. You went through something horrible. I can't imagine the things you must have seen. Must have done. But your family's not scared *of* you. They're scared *for* you. They don't know what to do to help you through this."

He shook his head, but didn't look away. "I close my eyes and I'm back there. It feels so real. What if I attack one of them in my sleep? I'm a danger to my family like this. I'm a killer. Like that girl at the hospital said."

She glared at him. "Stop that. You did what you had to do to survive. And no, you're not the same boy who left home a few years ago. You're a man. A man who's been through a war and made it out alive. So many didn't. And that's nothing to be ashamed of."

She wanted to scream at him, *What about the girl you saved?* If he were the monster he believed himself to be, he wouldn't have done such a thing. "I know it was difficult and you saw a lot of people die. But, did nothing good happen? Did you totally abandon yourself, or did you try to do the right thing?"

His gaze dropped to the ornament. "I suppose at least one good thing came from it." He slipped his hands out of her grasp and grabbed the ornament. "I made this from a gift I was given in Nam. It's supposed to grant my greatest wish."

She noted he didn't mention the fact he'd risked his life to save someone else in order to earn that reward. He wasn't about to boast, not even to sweet-talk a girl. Amazing.

"And what would that be?"

"To find someone I could love. Someone like you."

Her heart melted. She pushed him back onto the couch. His eyes widened and he opened his mouth to say something but she didn't give him the chance. She swallowed whatever he'd been about to say. She held herself above him, barely an inch of air between their bodies. Their lips the only point of contact.

The ornament landed with an audible *thunk* on the shag carpet.

ꕥ

Lee let out a little moan. His body strained up off the couch toward her. She lowered herself until her body covered his. One of his legs sandwiched between hers. She rocked against him and gasped at the feel of his erection pressed against her core. The cheap fabric of her pantsuit a weak barrier at best. His heat seared her. His hard length caused tingles of awareness to pulse up and down her body.

A shadow of unease slipped into her consciousness. This behavior was completely unlike her. What was she doing? She barely knew this man and here she was devouring him on his parents' couch. She buried her head in his neck to hide the blush that set fire to her face. How to explain that she'd gotten carried away?

His chest vibrated as he cleared his throat. He seemed to struggle to catch his breath when he spoke in a rough voice, "I—I think we should take this a little slower."

*So* not the response she'd been expecting.

"You…what?" She pushed up on his chest so she could get a better look at his face. There was that blush again. It seemed to come naturally to him. Maybe because of his fair skin.

Their position was awkward to say the least. The heel of her hand ground into his sternum and he winced. She jerked back to take the pressure off. Her lower half ground into his and she came up against the evidence of his arousal. His body wasn't calling it quits. So what was?

She slid off him, landing on her knees at the side of the couch. Her hand brushed his crotch. He groaned and pushed himself into a sitting position. He sat forward, elbows on his knees and head in his hands.

"I'm sorry. I want to. I can't begin to tell you how much I want to." He studied her with an agonized gaze then let out a long, whooshing breath. "But it's not right. I can't take advantage of you like this."

She laughed. "I seem to remember being the one on top. I wouldn't call that *you* taking advantage of *me*."

"Nevertheless. You're vulnerable. You don't know who you are, or whether you're even free to pursue a relationship with me." He stood abruptly. "And…"

She stopped listening. He was right. Well, not completely. She had no one at home. But she still wasn't free to pursue a relationship. Or was she?

He paced around the room. His leg brushed against the Christmas tree and set the ornaments tinkling. He ran a hand along the back of his neck as he stared at the lights.

"I'm sorry, Dani. I have no right to even think about a relationship with you. You deserve so much more."

"Bullshit."

He swung around. "Excuse me?"

"I said, bullshit." She leaped off the couch and faced him, poking a finger at his chest. "Yeah, you heard me right." She poked him again for good measure, pleased to see him wince. He needed the point pounded into him, apparently. "You're a good man. You're suffering right now. I get it. But don't for a minute think you're not good enough for anyone because of what a few whackos have to say about something they have no clue about."

He shook his head. "You're amazing. That wasn't just a line earlier, you know." He brought her hand to his lips.

Her heart fluttered and she lost her train of thought. "What line?"

"That you're my greatest wish." He plucked the ornament off the carpet. "I guess it's safe to give this to Tracy. I didn't need it after all." He turned her hand over and placed the ornament in her palm.

Her vision blurred. Dizziness washed over her while her stomach heaved. Her knees buckled. Lights flashed behind her eyes. No! She gasped and began to fall. She didn't want to go. Not yet. They needed more time.

"Dani!" He caught her before she got too far. He swept her up into his arms, carried her to the sofa, and lay her down gently. "I've got you."

The ornament fell from her grasp.

The world slowly righted itself. Her stomach settled, she breathed deeply, and the dizziness passed. She could focus on Lee's worried face.

The gentle glide of his hand across her cheek comforted her and she turned her face to kiss his palm. What had the old man said? He'd never needed the ornament because he'd already met his wife.

She belonged here. She wasn't going anywhere.

಼ೲ

Dani Russell sat back in her seat while her husband of almost fifty years flirted with a younger version of herself. Quite literally.

The little café looked just as she remembered. Of course it would. After all, she'd seen it last on this very day, before her little trip through time.

Ah, yes. There she went. Why she'd decided to stand up when she felt that awful, she had no idea. The thought of those first few moments after touching that ornament sent a shiver up her spine. She'd been overcome with dizziness.

The only thing she could compare it to was when she was pregnant with each of their four children. She'd barely suffered from morning sickness, but the dizziness had been overwhelming.

When Lee picked up their canvas shopping bag, she spotted the strap of her younger self's purse sticking out the top. *That wretch!* She'd always wondered what had happened to it.

She smiled when he turned and winked at her. Even the thick glasses couldn't hide the sparkle in his eyes. He'd deny it. Sparkle wasn't manly, after all.

The door swung shut behind her younger

self, causing a cold draft to shoot straight up her blouse. She struggled with the zipper of her winter coat.

It took him a bit longer than it would have in his younger days, but Lee shuffled over and shooed her hands out of the way. He zipped her up then patted an aged hand against her cheek.

"Ready?" he asked.

She took a deep breath and held it for a second before letting it seep out as she counted to ten. She nodded. "I suppose. I'd say I've had more than enough time to deal with my mommy issues."

He held out his arm. She used his strength to lift herself out of her seat with a groan.

"You'll be fine. Your mother might be a bit surprised, though."

She laughed. "To say the least. Last she saw me I was in my early twenties. Now I'm older than she is."

"She's still your mother," he said as they shuffled to the door.

"I know."

He stopped, dragging her to a standstill at his side. Exactly where she'd been ever since she first touched the ornament.

"Dani. Do you need more time?"

She shook her head. "No. We need to do this. We've paid up all the bills, and they're expecting her at that nice place we found. She'll be well taken care of—physically." *That's not enough.*

He patted her hand. "Now we need to take care of the rest."

"Yes. And I want to have one last Christmas with her. I want her to know the life I've led. That I've been happy. It will be my gift to her. I think she'll appreciate it."

"She will." He gave her hand a squeeze.

"I know. And I'm ready. Honest."

"You're still nervous."

"Yes. She's dying. I've come to terms with that. I've even come to terms with the way she raised me. I'm just a little nervous of her reaction to seeing me like this." She waved a hand over herself.

He placed a kiss on her cheek. "You're as beautiful as the day we first met." He cocked his head to the side. "Which is today, technically."

She laughed. "Thanks, honey. I can do anything as long as I have you at my side."

He grinned, raised her gloved hand to his lips, and placed a kiss on her wrist.

"Always."

About…

Emma Kaye is married to her high school sweetheart and has two beautiful kids that she spends an insane amount of time driving around central New Jersey. Before ballet classes and tennis entered her life, she decided to try writing one of those romances she loved to read and discovered a new passion. She has been writing ever since. Add in a playful puppy and an extremely patient cat and she's living her own happily ever after while making her characters work hard to reach theirs.

For more information on Emma, please visit her online at www.emma-kaye.com, on Facebook at www.facebook.com/emmakayewrites, or on Twitter at www.twitter.com/emmakayewrites.

Love time travel? Try another Emma Kaye time travel story—***Time for Love*** is available now from The Wild Rose Press!

## Time for Love

Alexandra Turner will do anything to save her twin sister. Even when she's transported back in time to Regency England. Rescuing her sister and finding her way back to her own time will take all her concentration. Falling in love is not an option.

With the death of his brother, Nicholas Somerville became the ninth Marquess of Oakleigh and must return to England to take his place in society. Part of his responsibility will be to find a wife. It never occurs to him he might actually discover a woman he could love—until he meets Alex on his voyage home.

Can Alex and Nicholas find a way to bridge the gap of time and circumstance? Can they overcome their fears to realize that true love transcends time? Or will a dark secret from Alex's past rear up to separate them forever?

# Letter from St. Nick

Nicole S. Patrick

Thad Sinclair is at a crossroads, but when he receives a letter informing him of an inheritance, the conditions force him to rethink his life's course. Will this war-hardened US Marine finally find a place he can call home?

Scarlet Madison's idea of a real Christmas can possibly come true this holiday. She just needs to prove that she can stand on her own two feet and save her gallery in the process. Can she realize anything is possible with unconditional support and love, no matter where it comes from?

An unexpected gift may lead Thad's and Scarlet's hearts to the same place.

Dedicated to ~

My wonderful partners—for your inspiration, friendship, guidance, and lots of laughs.

Joe and our boys—for your love and support. Yes, mommy is still busy writing.

My fantastic editor, Mallory Braus—for making this experience invaluable and fun too. Thank you for your direction.

# Letter from St. Nick
## by Nicole S. Patrick

"Last call for flight one eighty-nine, nonstop service to Jacksonville, Florida. All seats boarding."

Thad Sinclair groaned at the stiffness in his kneecap, the result of sitting too long. Twenty-four hours ago he'd left Afghanistan, flown to Istanbul, and was at the tail end of a six-hour layover in New York City. God, he was beat. Plus, he was a grubby, ripe mess in his cammies and combat boots. He grabbed his rucksack, following the other stragglers in line to the Jetway for the last leg of his journey home.

Wherever that was.

The gate agent smiled, thanking him for his service when she took his boarding pass. Many people had stopped him to say "Thank you" or "Welcome home" since he'd arrived at LaGuardia Airport. It was good to be back on US soil and see friendly faces instead of watching his back and fighting insurgents at every turn.

He stowed his bag in the overhead compartment, settled in his seat then took a creased and worn sheet of paper out of his shirt pocket.

Not two weeks ago, Lieutenant Grant had kidded, "Sinclair, here's a bunch of mail for you. What'd you hit the jackpot, my man?"

He sighed and shook his head.

Thad unfolded the letter and a sharp sting hit the back of his throat. Aw, hell. He blew out an unsteady breath as wetness seeped behind his eyes. His gut clenched just thinking about the man who had been more "Dad" than his own ever was.

*Thad, my laddie, if you are reading this letter it means that I'm gone. And it also means there are some things you need to be apprised of. My good friend and attorney Rupert Green has all the information for you about my estate.*

*It's time, Thad. Stop the globe-trotting and fighting the bad guys, and come back. Plant some roots, son. I'm just sorry I won't be here to greet you.*

*You are the son I never had. I've always been very proud of the path you took. To this day I think your father was a jackass for all the pain he caused you, rest his soul. I hate writing this sentimental drivel, but I figured your aunt Maeve would've wanted me to.*

*Not many people knew I was sick so don't go beating yourself up or getting upset over things. There was nothing you could've done. No use in fighting the inevitable. I'm going to join my Maeve now, and I'm okay and ready for it.*

*Semper Fidelis,*

*Uncle Nick.*

Thad slid up the window cover to gaze at the planes parked side by side in the terminal.

It'd been more than three years since he'd last seen his uncle. Yes, three years ago at Dad's debauchery of a funeral right here in New York. His parents' decision to leave what remained of their fortune to charity had turned ugly at the reading of their will. The Sinclairs were not a forgiving bunch. That was a fact. No, the stuffy, upper-crust, uptown cousins he couldn't stand looked down their noses at the soldier in the family. He'd given up years ago making the correction that he was, in fact, a *Marine.*

None in the Sinclair branch of the family tree had ever pardoned him for being the "disappointment" to his father, even after the old man passed away.

Uncle Nick and Aunt Maeve were the only family who'd accepted him despite all of his faults, shortcomings, and "unrealistic"—according to dear old Dad—aspirations. Thad never understood how unrealistic it was to want to serve and protect the country which helped shape the Sinclairs into their successes. Ironically, Nick had been a black sheep in the Sinclair clan too. Maybe that was why they'd become close before he'd shipped out to begin his stint in the Corps.

Thad racked his brain to recall any telltale signs in Uncle Nick's appearance the last time they'd met. But the strapping giant had embraced him with the same spine-cracking hug, kidding him about making nice with the rest of the family.

*Had* Uncle Nick been sick back then? Understandably, he'd been sadder since losing Aunt Maeve, and not nearly as animated as he normally was during the Sinclair family get-togethers. More like battles. But nothing else had seemed different.

He sniffed and swiped his eyes, sinking against the cool leather of his upgraded first-class seat. Damn! Why hadn't he reached out sooner? Why had he chosen to be gone for so long? Perhaps the day-to-day shit storm of war was what had held him back from at least sending e-mail? *What a lame excuse.* He could've found the time. The motives for staying away may have been valid at the time, but for some reason he couldn't recall any of them.

Now he'd never get to say goodbye. Talk about feeling lower than a junkyard dog. He'd wasted so much time *not* keeping in touch with the family who *actually* cared about him. His parents, for certain, hadn't given a flying… *Stop it, Sinclair. No use thinking about them now.*

He clenched his jaw and swallowed hard. Anger waned into the familiar ache of loneliness, as it always did when he thought of his parents. He tamped down the vise of pain surrounding his insides, just as he'd done eons ago when he was a young Marine.

He scrubbed a hand down his face and

placed Uncle Nick's letter on the vacant seat beside him. He closed his eyes as a headache crept up the base of his skull.

The thought of going back to active duty after this leave was over made him twitchy. He had to admit, the bum knee was shot, and someday he feared it just might get in the way of his survival. Maybe it was time to let the younger, gung-ho guys take over. Was he actually considering throwing in the towel?

*Focus on the now, Sinclair.* Once he arrived in Florida, it would be a quick trip to Jacksonville to get his truck from his buddy's garage and retrieve what remained of his scant personal belongings from the storage unit.

"We'll be taking off momentarily, folks." The pilot's voice cut through the speakers. The announcement, coupled with the engines firing up, jolted Thad out of his musings.

Two weeks ago he wondered about his next destination. Now he knew—Amelia Island, Florida.

ꟷ

The elevator opened to the fifth floor, revealing a door etched with the names Green and Madison. Suddenly, the breakfast he'd wolfed down on the drive onto the island lodged in his throat.

A pretty blonde looked up as he approached the reception desk, giving him a smile.

"Can I help you?"

"I'm here to see Rupert Green. I'm Thad Sinclair."

Her eyes widened. "Oh, Mr. Sinclair, I'll tell him you're here right away. Can I get you a cup of coffee or some water?"

As she came out from behind the desk, he took in her tight shirt and miniskirt.

"There are doughnuts in the pantry. But you don't look like the type who would ever touch one." Her eyes brightened with her smile.

She was kinda hot, actually, but no older than twenty-one at best. *Too young, Sinclair. Steer clear.*

The corner of his mouth lifted. "No thanks. I'm fine."

She escorted him to a room with floor-to-ceiling windows overlooking Amelia Island Harbor and smiled over her shoulder. "He'll be in shortly." The door clicked shut behind her and he turned to gaze at the busy waterfront.

What a difference a few days made. Here he was, clean and cool and safe, while the guys in his unit were still in the hellhole of Kabul, with its dusty streets crawling with insurgents disguised as merchants selling their wares at the marketplace.

His stomach roiled thinking about those left fighting to stay alive, day after day. He'd spent years trying to make sure his team was all accounted for by going out on every mission. He still couldn't enter a room without scoping out the exits first.

Christmas music piped in through the speakers in the ceiling, and the local radio station DJ announced there were only three shopping days left.

He leaned his forehead against the glass and closed his eyes. A shiver ran down his spine and his shoulders bunched as the phantom smell of sulfur and sweat and fear haunted him. He'd seen and done enough for a lifetime.

*It's time, Thad.*

He let out a heavy sigh. Perhaps it *was* time to move on.

"Mr. Sinclair?" He turned around and located the source of the deep voice—a man in his seventies, white hair and tanned wrinkles who wore a long smock covered with paint splatter.

"I'm Rupert Green." The man's eyebrows rose to his hairline. "My, but you're the image of Nick." Green extended his arm and his grip was surprisingly firm.

Rupert was right. He and Uncle Nick shared the same dark hair and green eyes and both were a few inches over six feet.

"A pleasure to meet you, sir." Thad arched an eyebrow. Was there blue paint in the lawyer's hair?

The man cleared his throat. "Pardon my attire. Our local artists' group meets every Tuesday," Rupert explained, "and I lost track of the time working on my latest creation. Do sit down."

"Call me Thad," he said, pulling a heavy chair away from the conference table and trying to stifle a wince as his knee screamed for relief.

"And call me Rupert." A questioning look flashed across the man's face when Thad eased himself slowly into the chair.

"I've got a bum knee."

"Oh, is it serious?"

"Serious enough, I guess. An IED, err, bomb blew up my caravan about a year ago and messed me up pretty bad." Images of the blast careened into his mind.

"I'm so sorry." Rupert sounded quite

sincere. "Funny your uncle never mentioned you'd been hurt, and he talked about you quite often."

A hot flush crept up his neck. "I didn't tell anyone about it," he mumbled. "Docs fixed me up, put some hardware in the leg, and I went back to my unit." Suddenly a thought struck, and he shook his head with a silent chuckle. Rupert eyeballed him like he was some sort of certifiable loon.

"It's just… How fitting, huh? Uncle Nick never mentioned he was sick to me, and I never told him I got hurt."

"Seems to me you two had a lot in common, and not just your outward appearance." Rupert smiled and Thad felt the beginnings of a connection with the older man.

Rupert sat in the chair directly across from him and placed a stack of files on the table. "Did the receptionist offer you anything? She's my daughter, Maria."

Thad forced himself to keep a neutral expression. "She did, but I'm fine, thanks." Rupert's eyes narrowed for a split second, making Thad hope like hell his face hadn't betrayed what he'd been thinking of cute, *young* Maria.

"Okay then, let's get down to business, shall we?" Rupert pulled a manila folder off the top of the stack. "I'm glad you received my correspondences. I was afraid it would take longer to hear back from you."

"Mail is slow overseas," Thad explained.

Rupert adjusted a pair of reading glasses on his nose. "Yes. It took me quite a bit of time to track down your unit. You are a hard man to find."

He shrugged. "Nature of my job and all. I got your letters, so that's moot, right?"

The lawyer regarded him over the rim of his glasses. "Absolutely moot. Thad, please let me start by saying how sorry I am about your uncle's passing."

"Thank you." Suddenly a basketball-sized lump formed in his throat. "Did he…" He cleared his throat. "You two were friends, correct?"

Rupert nodded. "Nick and I became close friends."

"Did he suffer?" The question came out in a whisper as he stared at the table, studying the swirls in the wood, dreading the answer.

"Your uncle's last days were peaceful." Rupert's expression was filled with nothing but compassion.

"That's good. Who went to his funeral?"

"Most of the locals paid their respects. The Sinclairs were true pillars in this community."

He tried swallowing, but it felt like an entire bag of cotton had taken up residence in his mouth. "They were both great people," he agreed. *Way to go, Sinclair. State the obvious.* The look of sadness that crossed Rupert's face made him pause. "I'm sorry for your loss too, Mr. Green. You know, Uncle Nick was the reason I became a Marine, so you're right about some things we had in common."

"So he told me." Rupert's eyes crinkled with his grin, erasing some of the sorrow in his expression. "Let's go over the conditions of his last will and testament." He handed over a multipage document and began to explain the legal jargon on the pages.

When Rupert finished talking, Thad could only stare blankly. "Let me get this straight. My aunt and uncle owned *this* much real estate?" He rubbed the back of his neck. "I thought Uncle Nick had a shrimp boat."

Rupert took off his glasses. "He did, and much more. Many big resort developers tried to get their hands on his stretch of prime waterfront property. But Nick refused to sell out. You see, he loved the local small shop merchants, many of whom are second-generation, and they depended on him too. I suspect they'll depend on you now."

Thad picked his jaw off the table. What, was he supposed to be a landlord now? He had a serious aversion to being told how to live his life. It was bad enough living with the guilt of knowing some of his men hadn't made it out alive, but being responsible for a "community" was not on his immediate agenda.

He straightened and looked the attorney square in the eye. "How about I be the one to figure out what's next for me, if it's all the same to you."

A slow smile appeared on Rupert's face. "Nick mentioned you were a hard one." He put his glasses back on his nose and continued. "In the absence of any children, the Sinclairs named you as their sole beneficiary and bequeathed their entire estate to you. There are conditions, though," Rupert added.

The little hairs on the back of his neck rose. He leaned forward. "What estate and what conditions?"

Rupert's placating manner was seriously getting on his nerves.

"The Sinclairs shared a palatial house, purchased right before your aunt passed away. It is yours provided you live on Amelia Island for a full six months and keep the leases on the properties.

This will give the shop owners time to buy you out if they can secure the funds, or, if you decide to settle here and keep things as is, you will receive the substantial monies in their bank accounts at the end of said period."

Thad's mouth fell open. "Why in the hell would they do that? I'm still in the Marines." Well, technically he *was* considering getting out the Marines, but no one knew of his plans yet.

Rupert put down his pen and pressed his fingers to his lips, choosing his next words carefully. "Thad, I don't know all the reasons. But I do know Nick missed you terribly. He didn't want you to worry about him. I'm sure you recall that salty-dog, former-Marine exterior of his," he said, sadly. "As I mentioned, we became close friends, especially when he fought to preserve the hometown feel and integrity of the island. Nick truly loved this place. Maybe he thought you would too."

There went the churning in his stomach again. Great. He felt like an idiot. They'd left him a fortune and he came off sounding ungrateful. So what if there were conditions—he could live with them and figure this out, right?

"Thank you, Rupert. I have a lot to be grateful for, it seems, and I absolutely appreciate you explaining things, sir."

"You're welcome, son." Rupert stood and Thad followed suit. "The keys to your home on Sycamore Lane are in the envelope." He gestured to the table. "Mr. and Mrs. Hanson take care of the house and grounds and will make sure you have everything you need."

Rupert then reached into the pocket of his

smock and pulled out a business card. "If you require anything at all, call me, anytime. By the way, our annual Christmas Eve party is in two days. Most of the local business folks attend. It might be a good way for you to introduce yourself and get to know them."

Thad nodded absentmindedly—trying to grasp so much information in so little time.

Rupert exited, but he barely heard the click of the door.

Everyone was gone now. Besides being with his brother Marines, he'd never fit in anywhere. Maybe it was his lot in life to be without a family. But why, suddenly, did the notion make his gut feel hollow?

*Plant some roots, son.*

Thad gathered the stack of papers and pocketed the business card. As he reached the door it flew open. He tried to step back in time, but the heavy wood clunked him on the side of his head, and whacked him in his bad knee.

"Oof!" On instinct, his hands shot out to steady himself against the table before his leg buckled. The papers scattered across the floor.

Someone—definitely female—gasped. "Oh! Are you okay?"

He rubbed his throbbing temple, willing away the stars swirling before his eyes, and cracked open one eyelid. "I'll live."

Eyes back in focus, he was prepared to give the culprit a piece of his mind about barging in like a tank. He looked down and blinked. Was everyone in the painting club around here?

"I'm truly sorry. I thought Rupert was in here." At least she *sounded* embarrassed.

She was a little bit of a thing, wearing a multicolored, paint-smeared smock, which reached past her knees but still gave him a view of her nicely shaped calves and flip-flopped feet.

Her hair was pulled into some wacky hairstyle, like a palm tree gone berserk.

But when her eyes caught and held his he forgot to breathe. They were a brilliant sky blue and fringed with insanely long eyelashes. Not the fake kind that some women glued on, but all natural. A rosy blush spread across her freckled complexion up to her sandy-colored eyebrows.

She was sexy in an adorable sort of way.

"It's no problem, ma'am." He felt an odd need to reassure her even though she'd done *him* the bodily damage.

Her eyes darted away from his. "Oh no. It's all my fault for barging in without knocking first."

Holy! Her voice was like silk running down his arms.

She bent, frantically gathering the papers in a sloppy pile, still blushing, and so cute his chest tightened. He knelt to help her and breathed in a whiff of her perfume. Not overwhelming, but rather fruity and clean, and absolutely feminine.

*Okay, Sinclair, settle down, man.* It had apparently been way too long since he'd seen any female out of cammies or a uniform.

She shoved the papers at him, hitting him midchest. "Here." She swung around and shut the door before he could utter another word.

Idiot! He'd let her leave without asking her name. Were his reflexes shot from a little bump on the noggin? He snapped out of the Twilight Zone, and limped out of the room toward the reception desk. No sign of anyone except Maria, who gave him a wave as he hobbled to the elevators. He pulled Rupert's business card out of his pocket and smirked. Maybe he would attend the Christmas party, if for nothing else than to find out who she was.

*Way to go, Scarlet,* she berated herself, hiding in the bathroom until her heartbeat slowed to a non-cardiac-arrest rate. Her eyes widened at the reflection in the mirror.

Oh God. She looked like one of those crazy monkeys on the cover of *National Geographic.* Her hair was in the midst of a static electricity party and she hadn't gotten the memo. She ran her hands under the water and tried to smooth out the rampant wisps.

What had possessed her to barge into the conference room looking for Rupert? Oh why couldn't she have waited until tomorrow to show him the final plans for the Christmas Eve party? And then, to practically knock down the brick wall of a man standing there? She rolled her eyes. Yeah. Real graceful. Her father constantly accused her of rushing into things headfirst. Admittedly, the almighty Jebb Madison was correct in this case.

She took off her smock and shoved it into her bag. God forbid her father spotted her visiting his office looking like an "artist."

*Focus on the party, Scarlet. You've got two days to make it spectacular.*

Waves of heat washed up her face and she breathed in deeply. A mere two days to finish transforming her antiques shop and art gallery into the best venue the Green and Madison annual Christmas Eve party had ever seen. Hopefully the exposure to Dad's lawyer buddies might drum up business for the flailing shop. However, the plan was turning out to be a mission she had more than a few second thoughts about taking on.

Her parents had complained from minute one about practically everything. The shop was too small, the guest list too short, and her mother's idea of Christmas decor was a fake white tree with silver tinsel and bling-bling everywhere. Atrocious.

Thank goodness Rupert and the late Mr. Sinclair were on her side and had fought for her vision. The party would be simple and elegant, like Christmas should be—all about families and customs. The dysfunctional Madison family had no clue about the concept. And now, especially with Riley starting to understand the true meaning of Christmas, she wanted to create her own holiday traditions for the both of them.

Time to get back to work. She peeked her head out the bathroom door and let out a sigh. Whoever the brick wall had been, thankfully he was gone.

"Hi, Maria." She placed an envelope on the desk as Maria typed on the computer. "Give this to your father please?"

"Oh, hi, Scar. No problem," Maria answered, smoothing down her tight shirt. Her D-cups were new according to local gossip. Rupert Green indulged his only child with everything. The most *she* got from her parents lately was the "you need to find a nice lawyer" speech.

Maria faced her with bright eyes. "Did you

notice the hottie?"

Scarlet's stomach dropped. Did Maria mean the brick wall guy? "Must have missed him," she lied. "Why? Who was he?"

"Just Thad Sinclair. The Sinclairs' nephew who inherited their entire fortune," she leaned over and whispered.

Scarlet's brain stopped functioning. Hottie. Sinclair. Nephew. She groaned. "Oh no." She'd just beaned the new owner of her shop in the head.

Maria's eyes glazed over. "I wonder if he's going to be at the party."

The phone rang, interrupting their exchange. Scarlet headed to the elevators and gripped the bridge of her nose. This was a nightmare. Maybe Mr. New-Millionaire Sinclair would be too busy to attend. She could only hope. Talk about making a good first impression on her new boss.

ꙮ

Thad drove his truck to his new home, cruising along Route A1A and passing rows of million-dollar mansions. Who would have thought a shrimp boat business would have turned into an empire?

It was a far cry from what he remembered from the last time he'd visited Amelia Island—before his first deployment. It must have been ten years ago, at least.

His deployments blurred one into the next. Being a commander *and* combat veteran with no wife at home, it'd been easy to volunteer for so many tours. Plus, he was compelled by a deep-rooted need to make sure the young guys were looked after. Maybe it was because in the early days he'd always had strong superiors looking out for him.

His thoughts swam to the faces of his buddies who had lost limbs or, worse, their lives. Yeah, didn't he just feel like the luckiest son of a bitch with a mansion and big bank accounts, when all their families had no fathers, brothers, sons, or husbands?

Maybe there was a way to help them now that he was stateside.

He took a few turnoffs, looking for Sycamore Lane, and pulled up to the address with a large iron gate. He dug out Rupert's instructions, punched in the key code, and headed down the cobblestone driveway. Ahead was a house with a white stucco facade and pink flamingos painted across the front door. He cringed, then shook his head and laughed. His buddies would get a hoot out of this.

He parked his truck in front and got out slowly to take in the full effect of his new home. Home, sweet home. Hopefully there was at least a cold beer in the fridge and a big-screen TV somewhere. Kicking back for the rest of the day to clear his head just might be in order.

He grabbed his rucksack out of the bed of the pickup and slung it on one shoulder.

The pink flamingos should have been the tip-off to what he might find *inside* the house. How had his uncle, the retired gunnery sergeant, actually lived in this nightmare of flowers and lace? And who was screeching?

"You get back here, you thief!"

His heartbeat kicked up a notch and he crouched into combat stance, leaving the door open behind him. Suddenly, a large blur of black-and-white spots hurdled straight for him.

Thad tensed and dropped his bag with a thud.

"Where did you run off to now, Fergus, you mangy thing," yelled the high-pitched voice, getting louder and closer by the second.

The blur was a Great Dane, bounding with gusto across the floor, its nails scraping on the wood. Thad's mouth dropped open.

Was that a cooked chicken in the dog's mouth?

Thad backed up as the dog skidded an inch shy of cross-checking him into the flowered wallpaper, but did not drop the bird.

"Nicely done," he admitted as the dog eyeballed him. Its gargantuan head came up to his midchest.

Then, the screecher appeared from around the corner, wearing a red kerchief and brandishing a rolling pin in one hand.

"There you are, you bloody bugger!"

Holy! The scene was like watching a bad English sitcom on the BBC.

The woman huffed and puffed as her ample form faced off against the beast. But the dog stood his ground. Although every few seconds he cast a glance Thad's way as if to garner support.

Thad shrugged. "You're on your own, buddy." The dog whimpered.

The woman gasped, perhaps just realizing he was standing in the room. Her eyes widened. "Mr. Sinclair?"

"That'd be me." He straightened and gave her a lopsided grin.

Her face turned beet red. “Oooh. Pardon me. How awful of me not to notice you there!” She glared back at the dog who slowly retreated toward the door.

“No you don’t,” she warned. The dog cocked his head to one side and seemed to give the warning a good measure of thought. But in the end, he bounded out the front door with great, lumbering strides.

Perhaps Fergus had the right idea.

“And here I’d planned a nice dinner to welcome you to your new home.” She threw her hands up and he ducked, fearing she’d hurtle the rolling pin at his head.

He took a deep breath. “Are you Mrs. Hanson?”

She laughed outright, probably from the horrified look on his face. “Well of course I am. Pardon the chaos,” she apologized. “That mutt is nothing but trouble, especially since Mr. S died,” she said sadly, shaking her head.

She picked his bag off the floor and closed the door with her foot in one fluid movement.

“I would’ve gotten it,” he stammered.

He watched in amazement as she snapped around on one heel, putting any drill sergeant to shame. She hefted his bag with ease and sauntered down the hallway.

“Of course you won’t,” she said over her shoulder. “Now follow me, laddie. It’s hotter than Hades out today. I’ve got a cold brew for you in the kitchen.”

A slow grin spread across his face. He just might like it here after all.

Hot and extremely bad breath wafted across his cheek and up his nose. He cracked open one eye and almost jumped out of bed. Fergus perched with his large front paws on the edge of his bed, panting, and drooling onto the pillow.

"Ugh. Get a mint, will you?"

The dog dropped on all fours. *Woof!*

Thad sat up then swung his feet onto the floor. The bedside clock read noon. He rubbed his eyes and stretched with a groan.

He couldn't remember the last time he'd slept as well. Must be the plush mattress and down comforter. A far cry from the dank cots in the makeshift barracks he usually caught shut-eye in. He barely remembered his head hitting the pillow last night.

However, if he continued to eat as much food as Mrs. Hanson insisted on filling his plate with he'd grow soft in no time. He patted his abs—happy to feel the paunch hadn't started just yet.

Although it *was* kinda nice to have someone wait on him and care about his well-being.

He looked around the room and wished he hadn't. The bright yellow walls covered in sunflowers were enough to blind him for life. Redecorating would have to happen, and soon. Wow, one night and he was already thinking of changing the place.

Fergus nudged his leg. A disgusting tennis ball covered in drool lay by his paws.

He ruffled the dog's head. "Let me at least hit the head."

The dog seemed to understand and sat back

on his large haunches, waiting patiently. Thad stood slowly, gingerly putting weight on his knee. Mornings were the worst until the stiffness subsided.

A high-pitched laugh came from outside. He limped to the window. A young boy was in *his* backyard—running across the grass, being chased by a yellow Lab.

"Go play fetch with them, Fergus," Thad suggested to his new best friend before returning to the view. His eyes narrowed and instincts born of years of training kicked in. The boy now lay motionless on the grass while the Lab barked and pulled at his shirt.

He quickly pulled on a pair of shorts and did his best to ignore the hot poker of pain radiating from his knee to his bare foot. He bounded down the stairs, through the kitchen, and out the back door.

Mr. Hanson, the elderly and small-statured groundskeeper whom he'd met last night, was knelt down struggling to help the child sit.

"What's wrong?" The boy, dog, and Mr. Hanson all looked up at him.

Thad flinched. *Way to go, idiot.* The boy leaned into the older man, who had put his arm around his small shoulders. Sure, the kid was probably terrified because *he* looked like a crazed lunatic charging bare-chested onto the scene.

*Note to self: Rein in the combat intensity, especially around kids.*

"Riley, this here is Mr. Sinclair." Mr. Hanson spoke softly and patted the boy's head. "He's St. Nick's nephew."

Thad frowned. "St. Nick?"

The white-haired man laughed. “That’s what he used to call your uncle, isn’t it, Riley?”

Looking a bit dazed, the boy nodded slightly. Then Mrs. Hanson appeared with a cup. “Here, lovey, drink this slowly. I’ve called your mom. Are you able to stand and come into the house now?”

“I don’t know. My legs are shaky,” Riley answered in a small voice before taking a sip.

Mrs. Hanson wrung her hands. “We’ll just wait a few more minutes.” Mr. Hanson got up slowly, also looking worried.

The Lab, glued to the boy’s side like a watchdog, wore a sash with a Diabetic Alert Dog emblem around its torso.

The situation became clear. He knelt beside Riley and held out his hand, palm up to the dog. The dog sniffed, then licked his hand as if to say he’d been given clearance.

“Hey, Riley, how about a piggyback ride into the kitchen? It’s a lot cooler in there. Plus, I need some company for lunch.”

Riley’s eyes shifted to his dog, and back to him. He nodded. “Kobe, come,” he ordered.

“Way to go, champ.” Thad turned around to give Riley his back. The boy hooked his hands around his neck and his short legs around his waist. “Hold on. Boy, you’re heavier than you look for a little guy.”

“Mom says I’m getting bigger, but I’m still not going to be a giant. She says good things come in small packages anyway.” Riley didn’t quite sound convinced.

Thad placed the boy down on a kitchen chair and took the seat next to him. “Your mom’s right.

When I was in Marine boot camp," he explained, "the small, wiry guys were always the best at the obstacle course. They could climb a rope better than most of the tall guys."

Riley's face lit up from his chin to his startling blue eyes.

Thad's eyes narrowed. Blue eyes, red hair…

"I learned to climb a rope at summer camp." Riley's chest puffed and his chin lifted. "But my hands got all blistered and Mom got upset." He shrugged. "It was fun anyway."

"Are you feeling any better, honey?" Mrs. Hanson asked Riley while handing Thad a steaming cup of coffee.

"You are a saint, Mrs. Hanson." He groaned at the strong aroma and took a sip.

"Sorry I worried you, Mrs. H." A blush crept up Riley's neck. The boy must somehow be connected to *her,* especially with his distinct coloring.

Mrs. Hanson ruffled the boy's hair. "It's okay, love. These things happen, eh?"

"Riley! Where are you?"

Strange shivers coursed down Thad's bare back. Even before she came into view, he knew the owner of the voice—paint-smock sexy lady. The door to the kitchen crashed open, apparently her trademark, and there she was. No sign of the smock today, just a pair of denim shorts and a white tank top accentuating every curve and muscle of her tight little body.

8003

Scarlet drove like a bat out of hell from her

waterfront store to the Sinclair house. She held her stomach with one hand, biting her lip until it hurt. Riley would be fine. These were the kinds of things they'd managed together since his diagnosis. Thank goodness for Kobe. At least her parents had done the right thing by footing the bill for his expense—Diabetes Alert Dogs cost a small fortune. But God forbid her parents ever *watched* their only grandchild.

She turned off the main road heading toward Sycamore. Could it be any hotter today? She blew her bangs away from her eyes and cranked the air conditioner of her compact Toyota.

One more day to complete the finishing touches on the gallery before the party and she hoped—no, prayed—the planets aligned and everything continued to run smoothly. If this party failed she didn't know what the future would hold. If business didn't improve, she and Riley might have to relocate. And Amelia Island was the only home he'd ever known.

Scarlet took a deep breath and ticked off the to-do list in her mind to help calm her frazzled nerves: the caterer was all set, the musicians were confirmed, and the enormous *real* Christmas tree was perched in its stand, waiting to be decorated with ornaments each guest was instructed to bring.

She parked crookedly and rushed into the mansion straight for the kitchen. As the door swung open, she did a double take and her mouth dropped open. Sitting beside her son, smiling and laughing—and bare-chested—was Mr. New-Millionaire Sinclair.

Shit! Scarlet closed her eyes, wishing the floor would swallow her up. Of course he'd be here.

He owned the place, for crying out loud. She hadn't thought about that when she'd dropped off Riley this morning.

"Mom!" Riley hopped off his chair and wrapped his arms around her stomach.

She breathed in his little-boy scent and offered up a silent prayer of thanks. He seemed okay. "Hey, big guy. Did you give Mrs. Hanson a scare?" She glanced at Thad Sinclair as he rose from his chair and approached her.

His eyes were a nice shade of green—like her Christmas tree—and he was much taller and bigger than she recalled from yesterday.

She might as well get this over with. "Hi."

"Hi. Again," he said with a lopsided grin that did strange things to her insides.

Riley broke away to fidget, which was his specialty. "Mom, Thad told me small guys like me are wired and can do lots of stuff big guys can't." His eyes sparkled and he was flushed—not in a sick way, but excited and happy.

Thad's gaze never left her face.

Heat rose up her neck. Damn her redhead genes.

"Wait, what?" She shook her head and looked at her son. "Wired?"

"What he meant…" The deep rumble of Thad's laughter made her flush even more. "…was wiry."

"Oh, right." She nodded. "I hope he wasn't a bother. Mrs. Hanson, well actually Mr. Sinclair, used to watch Riley for me whenever he was off from school. That's why he's here." *Way to ramble, Scarlet.*

His eyes widened. "Is that right? No, he

wasn't a bother."

The intensity in his gaze was a little unsettling. She broke their eye contact to reach into her bag. Perhaps checking Riley's blood sugar would help her concentrate on something other than Thad's bare chest.

"Let's see what's going on with your numbers, big guy." She made her way to the table, pulled the glucose meter out of her bag, and pricked Riley's index finger.

Out of the corner of her eye, she saw Thad flinch, and when she glanced up, he'd moved closer to investigate.

"Doesn't that hurt him?" he asked, concern filling his voice. The uncensored warmth in his eyes made her heart melt a little.

Riley answered first. "Nah, I'm used to it by now."

She smiled down at her big "little" man. "You're on the rise. I smelled Mrs. Hanson's Christmas cookies all the way from the front door. You can have some, but not too many."

Mrs. Hanson, who'd been milling around the kitchen, stepped forward, placing her hands on Riley's shoulders. "Let's bring some outside to Mr. H."

"Okay. Bye, Mommy. Bye, Mr. Sinclair." They headed out, Mrs. Hanson with her tray of cookies and Kobe following closely behind Riley. She bit her bottom lip and watched them exit.

"I'm Thad Sinclair, by the way." His voice dripped with amusement as he held out his hand.

She rolled her eyes but returned the gesture. "Scarlet Madison. I'm sorry about yesterday—you know, trying to kill you with the door and all."

He chuckled. "You're forgiven."

Suddenly her palms were super sweaty and she pulled away from his grip. "So, you moved in?"

He looked around the room shaking his head. "I guess for now. Interesting decor."

His expression was priceless. Here was this big, strong guy, a Marine from what she remembered Mr. Sinclair telling her, living in an ultra-feminine palace. She clamped her lips together.

"You find this funny?" He crossed his arms high against his chest, which made his biceps puff to astonishing size. God, she'd bet she couldn't get both hands fully around one.

Her eyes snapped from ogling his arms. "Actually, it's hilarious."

"Thanks a lot. I just can't understand how Uncle Nick stood for it." A sad light came into his eyes and his expression fell. He reached over her bag on the table and picked up a half-filled coffee cup.

"Well, he didn't *love* it. But Mr. Sinclair always wanted to please Mrs. Sinclair," she explained. "He once told me no matter what crazy thing she wanted in the house, if it made her happy, he'd do it just to see her smile. Now that's a love of a lifetime."

He glanced away and harrumphed. "I wouldn't know about that stuff." His voice echoed sadness with the admission.

"Neither would I," she added softly.

His gaze swung back to hers, but his expression was unreadable. "Isn't there a Mr. Madison?"

She snorted. "Just my father."

His eyebrows drew together. “Your father’s Mr. Madison, as in Green and Madison?”

“One and the same.” *Yes, Mr. Jebb Madison, lawyer extraordinaire, who put the* P *in pretentious.*

“What about Riley’s father?”

His question caught her by surprise. He was getting a bit personal, and quick. “You ask a lot of questions. Is that because of your new status?”

His lips thinned. “My new status? No. I was curious about *your* marital status.”

She blinked, suddenly feeling stupid. “Oh. Well, then no, I’m not married anymore,” she mumbled.

Time to end the awkward conversation. Besides, she needed to check on Riley and get back to working on the party.

Her stomach clenched. The party! Picking up her bag, she steered around him, making sure not to brush against his body.

“I’ve got to get going.”

But he moved in closer and blocked her path. He placed his hand against his heart. “Please don’t bail out on me now. I could really use decorating advice. And what’s this about my new status?”

The warmth of his large body enveloped her personal space. She tilted her head and focused on his eyes. Thad Sinclair apparently had a flair for the dramatic.

“Your status as my new boss.”

He rubbed his chin, alerting her to a very nice cleft under the hint of stubble.

“I run one of the shops on the waterfront for your uncle. Timeless Antiques and Art Gallery.”

Well, she was trying *not* to run the gallery into the ground. She hoped Mr. New-Millionaire wouldn't focus on the bottom-line profits anytime soon. The Christmas season hadn't been all that bad so far.

He frowned. "I thought you worked at the law firm."

"My father and Rupert own the law firm," she clarified.

He'd inched closer. "Interesting. Good timing too. My plan was to visit some of those shops today. Are you free?" His pupils were dilated, and his musky and definitely masculine scent made her stomach flip-flop.

"Free," she sputtered and her pulse spiked.

"Yeah, you know. Maybe you could show me around the town?" He raised his coffee cup then took a large gulp. The muscles of his neck flexed and she lost all train of thought. Why did he have to be such a hottie, as Maria had called him?

His eyes twinkled and he licked his lips, waiting for her to answer. She hoped he wasn't a mind reader. "Well, what do you say? I could use a pretty tour guide and maybe score an introduction or two."

Pretty?

Her mouth felt like the Mohave Desert and every nerve ending was on high alert—until Riley vaulted back into the room with both dogs in tow.

She backed away from Thad who quickly put his coffee cup down and began rubbing the back of his neck.

Mrs. Hanson followed behind, raising an eyebrow at her then sending Thad a curious look.

"Are you ready to go, big guy?" She herded Riley toward the kitchen door.

"No!" His little face was pinched and he stomped his foot, making Kobe and Fergus whine. "I want to stay."

Oh no. Getting Riley to leave the Sinclairs' house, and especially Fergus, had always been a challenge. He loved spending time with the Hansons too. She sighed, hoping to head off a full-blown tantrum, especially in front of *him.* "I think it'll be best to take you to the gallery. Don't you want to help me decorate for the party?"

"He *could* stay here, dear. You've got tons to do with the Christmas party planning. I'm sure we'll all be fine now," Mrs. Hanson assured her.

"Pleeease, Mommy," Riley pleaded, eyes wide, and her resolve melted.

"Okay. But only if you promise to be good and make sure to eat."

"Yes!" To her surprise, Riley skipped over to Thad and gave him a high five before running off with the dogs. She closed her mouth with a snap. Riley rarely connected with men, with the exception of Mr. Sinclair.

"*You're* planning the Christmas Eve party?" At her nod Thad added, "Rupert invited me yesterday. Why are you doing that if you don't work there?"

Her lips pursed. "The party is at the gallery this year. Why? Are you coming?" Now what possessed her to ask him? Was it because he was chiseled like granite and smelled great, or because he'd made Riley smile?

"What a lovely idea," Mrs. Hanson piped in. Scarlet was so focused on Mr. six-pack abs that she'd forgotten all about her.

Was he ever going to put on a shirt?

As she looked over, Mrs. Hanson gave her a knowing look and a wink.

He crossed his arms again and darted a glance back and forth between her and Mrs. Hanson. “Maybe. How about we make a deal?”

She blinked, not liking his tone and mentally running through the possibilities of what his *deal* could have to do with her party. Did he need a date? Doubtful. With his looks he probably had a girlfriend or a string of them somewhere. The thought made her stomach plummet for some reason.

“What did you have in mind,” she blurted out, then instantly regretted it.

There went that twinkle in his eyes again. “You’d never win at poker, you know.”

She cleared her throat. “Look, thanks for helping with Riley, but I’m pretty swamped today.”

He tilted his head and narrowed his eyes. “Don’t you think I have a right to see one of my stores?”

Now it was her turn to cross her arms. “Oh really?”

“Ahem,” Mrs. Hanson coughed and grabbed a dust rag before scooting out of the room. Scarlet lifted her chin and stretched to her full five feet two inches.

He crossed behind her but she refused to follow his movements. If he thought he was going to play the high and mighty Mr. Millionaire and make her cower, he was mistaken. She’d learned to deal with men who were full of themselves from the master—her father.

“You show me around the town, and I’ll help you with your party decorations,” he said in a low tone.

She spun around. “Are you kidding? Why would you want to do that?”

She expected the lopsided grin or snappy comeback, but he was staring down at his bare toes—which were nicely shaped—and shifting his weight.

When he finally looked up, there was a flash of vulnerability in his gaze that was so unexpected, her breath lodged in her throat. Her hand rose to her neck and she swallowed.

“Well, it seems I’ve got a lot to learn about this place and the people my uncle cared about. And you, Ms. Scarlet Madison, are the first merchant I’ve met. I figured, maybe if you’ll help me, I’ll help you.”

She let out a shaky breath and her knees turned to jelly. “You’ll have to put on some clothes first.”

He winked. “Be ready in five minutes.”

He surprised her again by leaning in for a quick kiss on her cheek, before he and his incredible smell drifted out of the room.

Lord, help her.

Scarlet led them to Jane’s bakery and café. Thad, complaining he’d missed lunch, insisted this was the first stop on their tour. As they entered the small shop, the aroma of fresh-baked bread and Jane’s famous chocolate croissants wafted up her nose, making her stomach growl.

“See, I knew you were hungry.” His low and sexy voice vibrated in her ear.

Most of the locals knew her and waved when she and Thad came in. Jane waved from behind the counter. A group of blondes with perfectly frizz-free hair eyed him like cool lemonade on a hot day. He seemed to ignore their ogling and focused his attention on her. But he was also scouting out the place, it seemed, by scrutinizing the front and back doors.

"Can we sit outside instead?" He pointed to a small table covered in red-and-white checked cloth out on the deck.

"Sure. Lead the way." She tried not to stare at his back end, but his tight T-shirt and cargo shorts fit his athletic frame like a glove. The man seriously had no body fat whatsoever. Maybe she wouldn't have dessert after all.

He winced slightly and favored one leg when he sat. Had she done that to him? "Did I hurt your knee with the door yesterday? Now I feel really bad."

His eyes swung back to hers. "Come again?"

"You grimaced when you sat," she clarified. "I'm really sorry. I can be a major klutz sometimes." *Great, Scarlet. Tell him all about your shortcomings. Way to make an impression.*

"You'll be hearing from the military lawyer tomorrow," he said and she couldn't read his expression. There was a tick in his jaw and his hands were clenched, resting on the table.

Her stomach dropped. "What for?"

"The lawsuit," he said flatly.

She swallowed hard. "Lawsuit?"

"Ms. Madison, you've done my body irreparable damage, and I may not be able to return to duty to serve and protect my country," he stated.

The color left her face. “Tell me you’re kidding.” She clenched her hands on her lap to stop them trembling. Maybe Rupert could represent her? Jeez, a lawsuit? What a mess.

Then she stole a glance at his chest and saw it rising and falling with silent laughter. Her eyes narrowed. “You’re playing me, aren’t you?”

The corners of his eyes crinkled. “It’s so easy to make you blush, I can’t help myself.”

“Very funny,” she huffed.

“Seriously, though,” he said, but the smirk was still there. “My knee has been a mess for a while. I had surgery about six years ago, then got reinjured during my last tour.”

She let out a breath. “Oh, good.”

“Good?”

“No, no,” she stuttered. “I mean, good that *I* didn’t do it. Not so good for your knee.” *Could* she be any more awkward around him? This was why she didn’t date.

She blew her bangs out of her eyes. “Why don’t we order? I *am* starving.”

Once Jane came to their table, she introduced Thad and they ordered. For a fit guy, he could really pack away the food.

“I remember this island being peaceful, like a little heaven on Earth. Have you lived here all your life?”

The sunshine backlit his face and his blue-green shirt accentuated the color of his eyes.

He put up his hand. “Wait. Before you tell me all about yourself, I just have to say something.” He leaned over the table. “Your eyes are amazing.”

She blinked. Red-hot heat coursed through her insides, making her want to fan herself with the tablecloth. "So are yours."

They smiled at each other in silence. Maybe he didn't think she was a dork after all?

"Well…" She bit her lip and fidgeted with her napkin. "I have lived here most of my life, except for college in New York."

"Ooh, big-city girl," he teased, but somehow she wasn't embarrassed or self-conscious about herself as she usually was sharing information. He was easy to talk to, when she wasn't blabbering like an idiot.

She laughed. "Hardly. I wanted to go to art school and there weren't any around here. I was accepted into the Pratt Institute, much to my parents' dismay."

He grinned. "Impressive. My parents both taught at Columbia."

Her eyes widened. "Wow. Did you get to go there for free?"

"Nah. I enlisted in the Marines right after high school, so there's no college on my résumé. Only the practical education of war." His words came out with a cynical bite. He gazed out over the harbor.

She had the sudden urge to smooth away the weary lines in his face, and take away whatever sadness had crept into his mind. Where had his easy grin gone?

The awkward silence dragged on. There was only so much soda she could drink to keep herself busy without having to use the bathroom. She started to push away from the table when he broke the silence.

"My parents had an antiwar mentality—the polar opposite of what I stood for by joining the military."

She nodded. "Ah, I see. You didn't conform. I can relate to that for sure."

He barked out a laugh, making the people at the next table look up. "Conform to corduroy pants and argyle socks?"

She wrinkled her nose. "I can't picture you in those."

"Not unless they make camouflage."

"Ha! I'll look it up on the Web and order you a pair for Christmas."

His eyebrows rose. "Thinking of giving me a gift already, and here we just met yesterday. I'm touched." He placed his hand over his heart.

So the lighthearted banter was back in full swing, but she suspected she'd hit a nerve and he'd merely pushed aside whatever hurt had surfaced. It was a defense mechanism she was very familiar with.

"Are you about done?" He nodded to her plate and cup. "I promised you some manual labor." He stood and offered her a hand.

She put her palm in his and smiled. "I hope you're ready to get dirty."

One of his eyebrows arched. "Dirty doesn't scare me."

ꟸ

"Wow. That's some tree." Thad looked up at what had to be at least a fifteen-foot Douglas fir. Not only that, but there were Christmas decorations everywhere and in no particular pattern. Like Christmas threw up and left in a hurry.

Scarlet sighed beside him. "It's wonderful,

isn't it?"

He scratched his head. "Well, it's *big.*"

She pinned him with a stare and he wanted to take back the words. Was she offended by his lack of oohing and ahhing?

Then she gave him a raspberry, which surprised the hell out of him so much he laughed out loud. He hadn't laughed this much in years. Scarlet Madison was like no other woman he'd ever met. There didn't seem to be a pretentious bone in her body.

He held up both hands. "What? I'm sorry. It's a great tree. Really it is."

"Stop. Just, stop," she told him and walked away, giving him a nice view of her swagger.

She came back and handed him boxes of lights. "I understand it's not everyone's cup of tea, so to speak, but *I* love it."

He searched her face, glad to see the smile still in her eyes. "Well then, that's all that matters, right?" *Sinclair, you are in foreign territory here, trying to placate a female.*

"Ha! Not if you're my parents, it's not."

"They aren't pleased with your choice?" he asked, almost afraid of the answer. She seemed a bit agitated now, dumping boxes of streamers and tinsel onto the floor.

"This tree," she began, "is a 'horror.'" She made quotation marks in the air with her fingers. "How dare I have a smelly, bug-infested thing at *their* party. Personally I love the scent of pine and evergreen. It's what Christmas *should* smell like."

"As opposed to…"

She whipped around and that crazy ponytail of hers was practically undone. His fingers itched to feel the softness of her hair. He remembered what it smelled like too.

"Oh I don't know." She shook her head. "Chanel, Burberry? Whatever the most expensive perfume is out this year." She stopped in front of him, hands on her hips. "Do you want to know why I offered up this gallery for the party?"

Was that a trick question? *Focus, Sinclair. Use your head.* "Because it was available?"

She rolled her eyes. "No. Because Green and Madison's Christmas Eve party is the go-to event of the holidays, and I have to drum up business for the gallery. I figured I'd play nice with my father's cronies and hope for the best."

She put the top on a plastic container and sat down with a sigh. "I have hated this party since I was five. Every year, my parents forced me to come to the over-the-top, horrible-food freak show. When all I ever wanted was to be in my footie PJs on Christmas Eve, waiting for Santa to come down the chimney and leave me presents. Maybe leave him some cookies and milk on the mantel?" She shook her head in disgust. "Nope. Never happened. Last year they tried to pimp me out to the next best and brightest attorney. Apparently, I need to find a nice lawyer and settle down to forget about my 'art thing.' As if I'd let any of those bozos near Riley." She sneered.

A rush of anger rose up and he clenched his jaw. No way was his Scarlet going out with some snot-nosed lawyer.

Wait a minute. *His* Scarlet?

"Where is Riley's father?" Hell, it'd been on his mind since she'd barged into the kitchen, so he may as well ask.

Her gaze darted away. "He bailed on us as soon as he found out Riley had diabetes." She shrugged. "Some men just can't handle it, I imagine."

"Actually, I can't imagine."

She looked up at him with an open mouth. "I believe that about you, Thad. You're a lot like your uncle Nick. He was a noble and honorable man. And he loved Riley and took care of him. He taught him to be brave. Riley's certainly the bravest six-year-old I know."

"Riley's a great kid." He didn't know many kids, but from what he'd seen of Riley, for a young kid he handled things in stride.

Her face beamed. "He is. But then again, I'm fairly biased." She laughed at herself.

She took a deep breath, which caused her chest to rise and fall beneath her tank top. His eyes zeroed in on the spot below her chin where a smudge of dirt hit the edge of her shirt.

"Back to work, I guess." She stood and bent to pick up the stray decorations.

He tried not to stare and pulled the collar of his shirt away from his skin. Boy, it was hot in here. *Get to work, Sinclair.* He ripped open the boxes of lights then started the monumental task of putting them on the tree to steer his mind away from *those* thoughts of Scarlet Madison.

What seemed like hours later, he carefully maneuvered down the ladder and stood back to view his creation. Hundreds of tiny lights twinkled on the tree, illuminating the room like tiny fireflies. He heard her gasp from behind.

"Oh, Thad, it's wonderful. Thank you so much."

He turned and she catapulted herself at him. On instinct, his arms wrapped around her tiny waist and he picked her slightly off the floor, pressing her body against him. He stifled a moan at her clean, fruity, and all-Scarlet scent.

She pulled away and he reluctantly put her down, unwrapping her from his embrace.

Standing before him, blushing and biting at her lip, she was sexy as all hell. God, why hadn't he just bent down and kissed her? *Lost your chance, Sinclair.*

She stepped back and waved her arms wide. "Ta da!"

He looked, wide-eyed at the transformation that had taken place while he was busy. "Nice job."

She inclined her head. "Why thank you." Looking down at her watch, she squeaked. "Shoot, I've got to get to the bakery before it closes and rescue the Hansons from Riley. Are you heading home?"

Something in his chest shifted. Home? He guessed he was kinda home—wasn't he? "I think I'll walk around and stop in the other shops for a while."

She frowned. "Are you sure?"

"Go," he said, taking her by the shoulders and turning her toward the door. "I'll lock up and have Mr. Hanson pick me up later."

She dug her heels in, causing him to bump into her back. Her head barely came up to his shoulders. She pivoted, got on her tiptoes, and kissed him.

His body stiffened and he closed his eyes at the shock of her soft lips against his. Lightning bolts of sensation shot straight to his toes. She swayed into him and her hands rested lightly on his chest. But the kiss ended way too soon.

When he opened his eyes, there was a mixture of flirting and insecurity in her gaze. "So are you coming to the party tomorrow night?"

A slow smile spread across his face. "I wouldn't miss it, Scarlet Madison."

"Now isn't that Scarlet pretty," Mrs. Hanson commented when he returned home.

"Beautiful," he answered without thinking.

"And that dear little boy. I do adore him," she continued, hefting boxes out of a hall closet. He jumped to help her and she pointed to the foyer table.

"She's a good mum, you know. It's too bad her parents are such awful folk." She shook her head, looking disgusted.

If he were smart, he'd steer clear of Scarlet Madison. Back the hell off, for his own good. *If* he got involved with her, would he be able to walk away in six months? Would he even want to?

Plus, she had a kid, a sick kid at that, *and* he owned her shop, for God's sake. There had to be some rule about fraternizing somewhere. What the hell did he know?

The only thing he *did* know was he'd never felt this level of pull toward any woman before.

Ever.

Scarlet Madison stirred up feelings and urges not exclusively of the "getting busy" kind.

"I assume you're going to the Christmas Eve party tomorrow?" Mrs. Hanson came up behind him.

He gave her a sheepish grin over his

shoulder. "You know I am."

"Good. I'll get your suit ready."

"How's that?" He didn't own a suit, except his dress blues.

She grinned and opened another box of Christmas decorations. "Well, while you were out, I looked at your size and purchased you some new things. The tailor is coming to alter the suit pants and shirt cuffs tomorrow morning. You'll look smashing for the ladies, or just one in particular, eh?" She winked.

"Oh, by the by, you'll need to bring an ornament to the party," she informed him. "I have the one your uncle wrapped up special," she added, sadly. "I'm sure he'd want you to bring it in his place."

"Take his place?" he asked halfheartedly. That didn't seem right.

She patted his arm. "There's no one else he would've wanted, laddie."

He watched Mrs. Hanson decorate and hum a Christmas tune and he sighed.

How could he honor his uncle's memory and those who cared so much about him, without feeling like he was replacing him?

Scarlet and the rest of the merchants had opened his eyes to so many sides of his uncle he'd never known. He laughed to himself. What had Riley called him, St. Nick?

Maybe there was a way after all. He'd have to call Rupert first.

"Mrs. Hanson. Save the suit," he said, heading for the stairs. He whistled for Fergus, who came bounding out of the kitchen. "Let's go for a ride, big guy."

ꕥ

The evening weather was perfect—cool and with little humidity, which did wonders for her hair.

"It's magical." Rupert stood next to her and surveyed the room with a proud look on his face.

She couldn't agree more. Her beloved tree was the centerpiece of the party.

All along the sidewalls outlining the various antique bric-a-brac on the shelves, tiny tea lights danced, their flames reflecting off the colors of the artwork hung on the walls.

"The silent auction for Juvenile Diabetes was a wonderful idea. Thank you for suggesting it." She squeezed Rupert's tuxedo-clad arm.

He winked. "Always looking out for a cause," he said then sighed. "Plus, if one of my pieces actually sells, it will justify all the time I spend away from home with you at the painting club."

"The painting club is what keeps us afloat," she commented.

"Things might look up for you soon, my dear."

What was Rupert referring to?

He gave her a quick peck on the cheek. "I must mingle. I see Maria and my wife beckoning for my attention. You look lovely."

She breathed in the aroma of peppermint and bayberry candles. Soft music wafted through the open gallery doors, and out over the waterfront as the string quartet she'd hired played Christmas favorites. It was elegant background noise for the guests as they milled around, drinking and eating the butler-passed finger foods.

She'd taken special care in getting ready tonight to make a good impression on any potential customers and also to please her parents. Unfortunately, her parents had already complained about the food and lack of "glitz" in her attire. Sighing, she grabbed a champagne-filled flute from a passing waiter.

Her hair was behaving nicely for once, swept up in an elegant French twist. And the simple, black spaghetti-strap sheath fit her perfectly. It was a comfortable choice, especially for darting around from guest to guest being a good hostess. The five-inch red heels, however, were killing her.

So what if her dress wasn't adorned with the sparkles of mother's full-length gown? Christmas wasn't about being showy. Christmas was about a feeling of warmth, and love, and family. Something hers would never understand.

But there was one person she hoped would understand. And one person she'd hoped to look special for. Thad Sinclair.

Who, as it happened, was not here yet?

A dreadful ache hit the pit of her stomach. Maybe he wasn't coming. Maybe she'd crossed the line with that kiss yesterday. She couldn't deny the connection with him—sizzling, yes, but also comfortable. What did she know? She and relationships never gelled.

She gulped down the champagne, placing the empty flute on a passing tray, and tried to steer her thoughts away from Thad Sinclair's smoldering eyes and easy smile.

"Merry Christmas," she heard from a passerby with his young son.

She smiled and looked down at the string

bracelet Riley had made for her in camp.

"Is that smile meant for me?"

Her stomach fluttered at the deep, warm voice. She looked up and lost all thought process. Her lips parted.

He looked amazing. From the gleaming gold buttons on his uniform down to his glassy shined shoes. His crisp white hat was tucked under one arm.

"You look gorgeous." He handed her a bouquet of flowers—big, beautiful poinsettias nestled into pine sprigs.

If he was sinfully handsome bare-chested, in uniform, he became extraordinary. He stole the breath right out of her lungs.

His eyebrows rose. "What, no thank you? And I'd hoped these were Christmas-scented enough for you. I'm crushed," he said with a twinkle in his eye.

"Why thank you, Mr. Sinclair. So nice of you to join us this evening." She tried to sound confident and aloof, but the wavering in her voice belied the effort.

His eyes narrowed. "Hmm. Ms. Madison, please accept my apologies for being tardy to your exceptional affair." He gave her a small bow. As a waiter passed, he took the bouquet from her and placed it on the tray.

Then he took her hands into white-gloved ones and brought them to his lips. His easy grin made her insides melt.

"Will you take a walk with me?"

She blinked. "What, now? Where?"

He chuckled. "Relax, Scarlet, it's just outside."

A blush rose up her neck and face and probably ruined her makeup. “I’d love to.”

He hooked her hand into the crook of his arm and frowned down at her. “You’re taller.”

She laughed. “It’s the heels,” she said, showing off her stilettos.

His eyes flared. “I like.”

They made their way through the crowd as people whispered behind their hands. A nervous laugh escaped. “I feel like I’m invisible next to you.”

“Not possible.”

Thad put on his hat and led them down the street to a park bench in front of Jane’s place.

He paced back and forth, seeming nervous, which was unlike him. Well, at least unlike the Thad she’d known for two days. Only two days and the pull of her heart toward him became stronger by the second.

He finally stopped directly in front of her. “You did an awesome job tonight. It looks amazing in there.”

Butterflies fluttered in her stomach and her mouth went dry. “Thanks. Your help meant a lot.”

He sat beside her but she didn’t meet his eyes; instead she focused on the razor-sharp creases in his pants.

“I hadn’t seen Uncle Nick in over three years, not since my dad died,” he began.

Her heart clenched hearing the pain in his voice. She took his hand in hers and looked up at him. “Tell me.”

He swallowed hard enough for his Adam’s apple to bob. An urge to lean in and kiss the spot rose up. *Focus, Scarlet, focus.*

He sighed. “Uncle Nick was the reason I joined the Corps. I wanted to be just like him. My relationship with my parents was already in the shitter.”

She laughed. “I can relate to that.”

“I’d spent this incredible summer here right before college and he taught me so much. Things Dad never considered worth a damn—like how to shoot and work his shrimp boat, and get my hands dirty fixing engines.” A bitter laugh escaped him. “My dad’s idea of dirty was reading a dusty manuscript holed up in the Columbia University library.”

“He sounds a lot like my father,” she said.

His shoulders slumped a bit and he pulled his hand away. “But then I ditched Columbia and enlisted.”

“Oh boy. That must have gone over well?”

“Not by a long shot,” he clipped. “Mom cried, which was her normal reaction to everything, and Dad shut down. After that they basically wrote me off. Never sent any letters or packages while I was in boot camp or overseas. It was tough being a new Marine and missing home something fierce. Aunt Maeve never missed my birthday, though,” he said with a small smile. “I guess I got hardened to the pain of their rejection after a while. I’d never fit in with them anyway. War hardens a person too, which is why I stayed away from here, I guess. I hadn’t felt fit for civilization or being around normalcy for a long time.”

Her heart hurt for him. “Thad, I’m so sorry.”

“Hey, I’m not looking for a pity party here. There’s a point I’m getting to, although not very well.”

"Take your time."

He puffed out a long breath. "So when I got this incredible gift from Uncle Nick, I felt like I totally didn't deserve it. Like I let him down by being so out of touch."

"I'm sure he never felt that way," she assured him. "In fact, he was very proud of you."

Thad swallowed hard again, and his eyes glistened in the evening light.

Okay, it was official. Her heart was his.

He chewed on his lip and nodded. "He said as much in his last letter. But knowing that still doesn't lessen my guilt. I mean, Scarlet, so many of my buddies will never see another day, let alone this kind of lifestyle." He gestured to the waterfront. "Hell. I'm talking forever here, right?" He looked down at his shoes.

He was so confident one moment, and so vulnerable the next. An incredible and sexy combination that made her want to caress the frown off his face and kiss him until he told her to stop, which she hoped was never.

"So the point of all this is, I want to give back, in his name. He gave me the greatest gift, unconditional love and acceptance for who I really was, and supported me in who I turned out to be."

He pulled out a document from his uniform pocket and held it out for her.

Her brows furrowed. "What's this?"

His eyes were determined. "It's the deed to your store, free and clear. For you and Riley."

Her eyes blurred and she covered her mouth with her hand. "Oh my God. Are you sure?"

"Absolutely."

She sniffed. "You have no idea what this

means."

"I think I do. I see how much the gallery and this island mean to you. But there's something else," he added with a smoldering look.

A flutter started low in her belly.

"I've decided not to re-up once my leave time is done. I'll have to go back to start the formal discharge process, but I am coming home. This place feels more like home in two days than anywhere I've been in the last fifteen years."

Tears formed behind her eyes. "I'm really glad you feel that way."

"Oh, and I talked to Rupert about setting up foundations with all those zeros, for kids like Riley and the kids my buddies left behind."

"You've been busy."

He looked uncertain. "Will you be here waiting when I get back?"

She threw her arms around his neck and held him tight. "Absolutely," she said and kissed the side of his neck.

His strong arms came around her waist and he pulled her against him. He was warm and hard and she heard him moan softly. He pushed her away to cup her face in his hand and lightly ran one knuckle down her cheek.

"You are beautiful."

She closed her eyes, savoring the feeling, craving more.

"Look at me, Scarlet."

No. Keeping her eyes shut was probably best. Then he wouldn't see how much he affected her. Maybe it was too soon? *No impulsiveness allowed. Step away from the hunky Marine.* Was she crazy? He was honest, and honorable, and he wanted her to wait for him. There was no way she was letting this go.

She felt him cup her head and tilt it back and her breath caught. “Look at me,” he repeated softly.

After another brief hesitation, she did. “That’s my Scarlet.”

His kiss, starting off gentle and tentative at first, intensified, bringing out a moan from deep in her throat. His lips were incredibly soft for a big, hard guy. Sliding them across hers again and again, he opened her mouth more fully and explored her tongue with his. One hand moved from the back of her neck, over the curve of her shoulder, and down the length of her spine. Her skin sizzled along the path of his touch.

“Scarlet, are you out there?” someone called.

He groaned and broke the kiss, but kept the brim of his hat against her forehead. “You’re missing your party.”

“I’d rather be out here with you,” she said, all breathy.

“Me too, but you deserve this night.” He stood and offered her a hand.

She stood, teetered on her heels, and took a deep breath. “Let’s go. The ornaments need to be hung on my tree.”

He tipped his hat. “Lead the way, ma’am.”

Once they went back into the party, Scarlet was pulled in all different directions.

Thad mingled amongst the guests, too, but she made sure to be at his side as much as possible. Each time she was, he put his hand on the small of her back and caressed her spine, making her feel like they were a couple. Even her parents made polite conversation, which was a shocker.

Thad patiently listened to them and nodded at their droning, superficial conversation. She was done trying to impress them. This party proved she *could* be a success in her own right, and Thad helped her to see that.

When it came time to hang the ornaments, she made her way to the microphone and called each person. Thad stood next to Rupert, watching her with all kinds of promise in his smoldering eyes. Her heart did a little flip.

When it was Thad's turn, all heads turned as he unwrapped his and hung it on the tree.

Her breath caught and she felt the color leave her face.

"Scarlet, are you okay?" He gripped her elbow.

She swallowed and blinked at the place he'd just vacated by the tree. "That ornament—where did you get it?"

He frowned. "Mrs. Hanson gave it to me. It was Uncle Nick's to bring. I hope you don't mind that I didn't buy one myself."

She grabbed his arm and shook her head. "No, no. Your uncle gave *me* the same ornament to put on the tree for *him*...in case he wasn't here for Christmas."

She reached for one of the lower branches and pulled off her ornament.

"Look." She showed him the match to his, a set of antique lovebirds painted in brilliant robin's-egg blue with flowered eyes. Her ornament looked to be the girl bird, and when she turned it over she gasped. Scratched into the bottom was *Maeve.*

"Let me see that one." Scarlet pointed to the

match. Thad reached up, pulled it off the branch, and put the small bird in the palm of her hand. There on the bottom was *Nick.*

Rupert barked out a laugh from behind them. "That old salty dog. Matchmaking from the grave."

"Unreal," Thad said, shaking his head. He wrapped her in his strong arms and she felt a sense of home.

"Wanna come over tomorrow for Christmas with me and Riley? You have to wear footie PJs."

He laughed, leaned down, and whispered in her ear, "There's no place I'd rather be."

About…

Nicole S. Patrick has always loved to read, and in her teenage years, she "borrowed" her mom's books to sneak away and become lost in the world of romance. After more than ten years in the corporate world of tech recruiting and HR management, she decided to stay home and raise children. But with so many romantic stories and characters floating around in her head, when the kids napped, she was compelled to put those words on a page and pursue this crazy dream of becoming published. Nicole writes romantic suspense and her heroes are those alpha males in uniform. She lives in New Jersey with her real-life hero, her husband, and her two sons.

For more information about Nicole, please visit her website at www.nicolespatrick.com.

Coming soon from Nicole S. Patrick…

## A Matter of Honor

A romantic-suspense novel about a Marine Corps captain and a traumatized investigative journalist—the daughter of the man he blames for his father's death. One of the core values of being a US Marine—honor—is tested as he is forced to help her solve a murder and do the honorable thing by keeping her safe.

# Secret Santa

Julie Rowe

A nurse grieving the death of her twin brother receives an unexpected gift at the staff Secret Santa party: the bullet that killed him and a message of hope and love.

Dedicated to ~

Hospital ER staff everywhere. You're all heroes.

George, my husband and best friend.

Mallory Braus, my editor, for her insights and suggestions. You're awesome!

# Secret Santa
## by Julie Rowe

"I hate Secret Santa," Kenzie Bowman muttered to herself. She crossed her arms over her chest and leaned against the wall, as far away from the crowded hospital's emergency department lunch room table as possible. The table was covered in wrapped boxes and gift bags. A bevy of nurses rummaged through them looking for their name on a tag, squeals of glee and laughter filling the remaining space in the room.

Anyone walking by would think it was Black Friday. They'd be lucky if they didn't end up treating one of their own for a bloody nose.

She used to love Christmas. The decorations, buying just the right gift for a friend, singing carols, and spending time with the people she loved.

Until last year.

Until her twin brother, Kennon, was killed on Christmas Day.

Now, she just wanted the entire event to be over. She never wanted to see another Christmas tree, hear another Christmas song, or taste eggnog ever again.

Her friend Amy surfaced from the circling sharks with a gift in each hand. “I found yours, Kenzie,” she said with Christmas cheer that darn near dripped sugar.

Oh joy.

Amy bounced up to Kenzie and thrust the gift into her hands, then proceeded to rip the paper off her own.

“Ohh,” she squealed, segueing into a victory dance as she hoisted her booty into the air. “A bottle of Baileys! Santa loves me, yes he does.” Amy paused mid-dance to lever her laser-sharp gaze at Kenzie. “Your turn, Ebenezer. Open it.”

“What’s the point? I don’t wear perfume, I don’t like scented candles, and I don’t drink alcohol. We know the likelihood of one of those three items being in this box is eighty-six-point-three percent.”

“You sound like a computer when you talk that way,” Amy said, enunciating each word individually.

“Better than having your eardrums blown out by indiscriminate screaming.”

Amy’s eyes narrowed to two slits. “Open the box.”

“Have I mentioned how much I hate Secret Santa?”

“The box, Kenzie. *Now.*”

“Fine.” Kenzie rolled her eyes and picked at the festive paper. “But if this gift sucks it’s going home with you.”

Amy's fierce expression slowly turned into a frown. "You don't just hate Secret Santa, you hate Christmas, don't you?"

"Do you blame me?" Christmas was supposed to be a time of joy and love, spent with friends and family. All that was impossible for her now. She and Kennon had been all each other had for eight years now. A heart attack had taken Dad from them. Mom followed him to the grave four months later.

Amy glanced away at the crowd of nurses and doctors for a second, then met Kenzie's gaze. "I suppose not. But it's not healthy for you to brood." She watched Kenzie's fingers as they slowly peeled the tape from the paper. "Come to my place Christmas Day," Amy said, the words rushing out of her mouth like a five-year-old who'd had too much candy. "Don't stay home alone. Please."

"I won't be good company."

"That's why you should come."

The last of the tape came off the paper and Kenzie carefully folded it and threw it into the garbage can. The box in her hand was too small for a bottle of Baileys, so it was down to perfume or candles. She opened the top, pushed aside the tissue paper, and pulled out a glass ball about the size of her fist.

The glass was plain, no decoration or sparkles. Something hung inside it, tied up in some string. She turned the ball to see if she could get a better look—

A bullet.

A smashed, wrecked bullet.

Pain seized her diaphragm and brought her breathing to a screeching halt. The agony ricocheted through her body until even the tips of her hair hurt.

"What's that?" Amy asked, staring at the ball, confusion furrowing her forehead. "It's not very festive looking."

It could only be one thing.

"The reason why I hate Christmas." Her voice sounded strangely calm.

"Huh?"

"This isn't from staff, it's from my brother's best military buddy."

Why? Why would he do this? Give her the one thing guaranteed to rip her heart out while it was only barely still beating.

"It's the bullet that killed my brother." The words came from far, far away. Almost an echo.

Amy's gaze jerked up to meet her own. "Your brother? But I thought he… Shit," she breathed out as a whisper. "How do you know it's *that* bullet?"

"Because he tried to give it to me before."

"He *what?*"

But Kenzie wasn't listening anymore. She was drowning in sorrow. It clouded her mind, sight, and hearing, pulling her under into a dark and silent world. Somehow she walked from the lunch room to the waiting room, but she had no memory of doing it. This must be what teleportation was like. Going from location to location without the inconvenience of conventional travel.

People turned as she entered the waiting area, most of them likely hoping she'd call their name.

Except for one.

One man stood slowly, staring at her face, his gaze apologetic. He was tall and fit, with a squared face that was strong rather than handsome. Every woman in the room turned to stare at him, but he didn't seem to notice. His whole focus was on her.

She angled her head back sharply then turned and walked a little ways until she got to a large wheelchair-accessible washroom. She went inside. He followed her in and she shut and locked the door.

Kenzie glared at the man who had been trying to give her a damaged bullet for the past three months. A man she'd refused to see again after their first disastrous conversation. A man she'd told to go to hell.

A man she'd once thought she loved.

Gage Remington.

She held out the box to him. "I don't want this. I never wanted to see it and to find it in a glass ball pretending to be a Christmas ornament—" For a moment she ran completely out of breath. "Take it."

He made no effort to accept the box. "Damn it, Kenzie, he wanted you to have it."

"My brother wanted me to have the bullet that *killed* him?"

"No. He wanted you to have a reminder of what you have to live for. 'We're all just a bullet or a breath away from oblivion; don't waste yours'—wasn't that the phrase you used to say goodbye with?" He took a step toward her. "He made me swear. It was the last thing he said to me before—"

She thrust a warning finger an inch from his nose. "Don't say it." She paced a step or two away, then back. "I never knew how stupid and childish it was to say the rhyme our grandfather taught us until the damn bullet showed up." She shoved the box at him and spun, grabbing for the door handle, but he got there before she could get the door open.

He took her shoulders into his hands and turned her.

She didn't want to see him, didn't want to touch him, didn't want to face the reality of her life with her brother—her best friend—no longer in it.

She pounded on Gage's chest and fought to get herself free.

He simply gathered her up and pulled her into his intractable embrace. Someone was crying deep, shuddering sobs that sounded like they were coming out of the throat of a tortured person.

That's when she realized—she was the person crying.

Gage whispered in her ear, "It'll be okay. I've got you now," over and over again as he rocked her. Her face was buried in his chest and his familiar smell made her cry even harder.

She'd missed him. Missed their conversations that covered every topic, conversations that often ended in argument. Missed their movie nights, when Gage and Kennon would tease her about her love of horror movies.

*Kennon.* She'd never get to experience any of that with her brother again.

He was dead.

Dead because he'd gotten in front of a bullet aimed at Gage.

Gage, her brother's best friend and her secret crush. All she could feel was guilt now when she looked at him. Guilt because he was alive and part of her was fiercely glad. The rest of her couldn't forgive herself for feeling that way.

So she cried.

Gage cried with her.

She wasn't sure how long the two of them wallowed in their sorrow, but it was long enough for someone to pound on the door. Amy, from the sound of the concerned voice asking if she…they were okay.

Kenzie pulled out of Gage's embrace, which was a lot harder to do than she expected, and opened the door. Tears blurred her vision and she was sure she looked like someone who'd been hit in the face with a dodge ball.

"Kenzie? Are you…all right?" Amy's wide-eyed gaze jumped between Kenzie and the tall, broad-shouldered man behind her.

"Not really." She sighed. "But when has that ever made a difference? Give me five minutes and I'll get back to work."

"No problem. I just wanted to make sure…" Amy retreated, closing the door as she went.

Kenzie stared at the door for several long seconds trying to figure out what she was going to say to the man behind her. Finally, she turned around with not an idea in her head.

Gage's eyes were bloodshot and his face as wet as hers. The front of his sweater was damp. She glanced at the mirror and discovered she looked even worse.

"Wow, we look terrible."

Gage heaved a huge sigh. "Always the realist."

"I really, *really* don't want to think about my reality right now. I have four more hours to go in my shift."

"I'm sorry." Gage said the words with a

deliberation that told her he wasn't apologizing for following her into the bathroom.

"I know." She struggled to speak around the gravel in her throat. "Doesn't make it any easier, though."

"Yeah."

Kenzie grabbed a couple of paper towels from the dispenser, wet them with warm water, and cleaned up her face. "You've given me the box with the…the…thing he wanted me to have. You've said you're sorry. Are we done?"

He nodded. "For now."

"What else is there?"

"I have a story to tell you."

"A story?" She shook her head. "Gage, I'm barely holding myself together. The story is going to have to wait."

"It can," he said, his tone telling her in no uncertain terms that he wasn't giving up, he was just giving her a little time. "Ken didn't leave things to chance."

She frowned. "Are you saying he made arrangements in case he was…?"

"KIA? Yes. We all did."

"I see." She nodded. Paced. Nodded again. "All right then. I'll call you when I'm on my days off."

"Kenzie…" His voice trailed off.

"What?"

"Take care of yourself." He said it like he meant it.

She wanted to tell him that the whole idea was ludicrous, but managed to say, "I'll try."

It was the best she could do.

ഇൽ

The ER was a place of feast or famine. Either they had more patients than chairs in the waiting room or there wasn't a soul in the place. Christmas Day was no exception, and it was standing-room only.

One of the local hotels had hosted a Christmas party the night before for three hundred people who worked for a construction company. Three-quarters of them were in the ER with all the signs of food poisoning. Hospital staff were handing out barf bags like crazy. If they had many more patients come in with severe vomiting, they were going to have to hit up an airline for more.

The adults were mostly fine. Medication to control the nausea was all most of them needed, but a few small children had been affected and they needed fluids in addition to medication. It didn't take a four-year-old long to get dehydrated when they couldn't keep anything down for twelve hours or more.

Kenzie found herself tired, fading fast and in charge of an intravenous assembly line. So far, she'd established IVs and began pushing fluids into four kids under ten years old, two ladies in their fifties, and three men who looked like they worked outside a lot. As she finished the last one, the ER doc handed her the chart for another child—a three-year-old this time.

"You're going to need another pair of hands to hold this guy down," Dr. Barry said. "He's not a happy camper."

"Thanks." She was so tired her voice sounded like an old car motor on its last mile. "I'll see if I can find some help."

The doctor shook his head. “Good luck with that.”

Kenzie went in search of another nurse, but everyone was busy with emergencies of their own.

She walked through the waiting room on her way to the small alcove where her patient and his parents waited, and spied Gage talking to one of the triage nurses. She was smiling and nodding to something he said. The nurse touched his arm in a way that told Kenzie she was very interested in sharing some “Christmas cheer” with him.

That sight sent a jagged arrow of protest through her, strong enough to have her walking toward them—to do what, she wasn’t sure—but letting the other woman touch Gage as if she had every right…

Kenzie stopped cold.

She was jealous.

No, no, no, she couldn’t be, but the fading anger wasn’t a figment of her imagination. Guilt, so cold it cut deep into her heart, doused the anger as if it had never been. How could she be jealous of another woman’s contact with Gage today of all days?

As if he’d heard her thoughts, Gage glanced up, and she found herself unable to look away. It was as if they were tied together by invisible ropes of the strongest steel. His gaze held hers for two long seconds, then he said something to the other nurse and began striding toward Kenzie like there wasn’t anyone else in the room.

Kenzie actually took a half step toward him before she could stop herself. She should go—she had a patient waiting for her—but he got to her before she could leave.

"What are you doing here?" she asked.

"Looking for you."

"I'm working. Didn't I tell you that yesterday?"

"Nope. You said you'd call on your days off. I didn't realize until after I'd left that I forgot to ask when those were."

"Oh." She hadn't told him for a reason, but now that he asked she couldn't find the energy to lie. "I'm off for a couple of days when tonight's shift is over."

"Why didn't you tell me that?"

She cocked an eyebrow.

"You're not going to avoid me, Kenzie." He leaned a little closer. "I'm very good at hunting people down who try to do that."

"I believe you." She took a step back. "We're slammed right now. I might even work a couple of hours of overtime."

"Can I help?"

"I wish. We could use you, but I'm afraid the powers that be don't like people walking off the street and lending a hand."

"When is your shift over?"

"I've got three hours."

He nodded, gave her another hard look then moved toward the exit doors.

Kenzie watched him leave, then headed over to the triage nurse who had hit on Gage. Just the person she was looking for. "I need some help with a three-year-old."

The rest of her shift went by in a blur of taking vitals and setting up IVs. She was still doing her charting when one of the other nurses paused at the station. "There's a guy asking for you at the triage desk."

"Tall, buff, and handsome?"

"Yep."

"Thanks." She didn't look up from her charts.

"You going to keep him waiting?" The nurse sounded surprised.

"I have to finish these reports."

"He doesn't look like the patient type."

"You'd be surprised." The thing was, she didn't know why he was here, waiting for her, in the first place. He said he had a story to tell her, but that could wait.

Today was not a good day for stories.

The nurse chuckled and walked away.

Ten minutes later a large shadow leaned over the desk. "Going to be long?"

Kenzie looked up into Gage's face and knew she wasn't going to be able to avoid him. "I don't know, maybe another ten or fifteen minutes."

"Can I wait here?"

She blinked. "Um, I guess." She cocked her head to one side. "Why aren't you spending today with your parents? Your sister and her kids?"

"I was with them this morning. The kids opened their gifts and we had turkey for lunch. Tonight I want to spend with a friend."

*A friend.* Well, what did she expect, that he would declare his undying love for her?

"I suppose I don't have a choice about that?"

He gave her a little grin. "Nope."

"Fine. Grab a seat over there." She pointed at a chair outside one of the patient cubicles a few feet away.

Gage moved with a feline grace that drew

the eye of most of the staff hanging around the nursing desk, but the only person he made eye contact with was her.

For a moment she couldn't breathe. Why on earth would this tall, strong, good-looking man be hanging around waiting for her? Because of his friendship with her brother? Or was there more to it?

Ridiculous. Happy endings were for romance novels, not real life.

In real life, bad things happened to good people. Period. Any fantasies about Gage professing his love, or any other fuzzy feelings for her, were just that. Fantasies. Fiction. Stuff that was never going to happen. She'd given him hints, but he'd ignored every one.

She needed to get that through her head before the last few intact pieces of her heart got stomped on. She'd hear the man out, then get him out of her place before she could do something stupid like tell him that he starred in every one of her fantasies.

Kenzie closed the last chart, put it in the completed pile then glanced at Gage and nodded.

He followed her out of the building.

"I live about ten minutes away," she told him.

"I'll follow you."

She got into her car and drove out of the parking lot, Gage in his vehicle right behind. She parked in the lot outside her apartment and they met at the back door. She didn't talk to him until the door was closed behind him. Even then she didn't look at him, just dumped her coat on a chair and kept walking.

"Coffee?" she asked.

"Sure."

She disappeared into the kitchen.

"No Christmas decorations," he said from the living room.

"No."

He didn't say anything for a couple of seconds, then commented, "Christmas happened anyway, though."

She flinched, but managed to say in an even tone, "That it did." She poked her head around the wall separating the kitchen from the living room. "Hungry?"

"Only for conversation."

Too bad.

She smacked herself on the forehead. That was not an acceptable thought.

She brought out his coffee and a cup of tea for herself and set them on the coffee table. She sat on the couch as far away from him as she could get. It wasn't far enough. Gage was a big man—over six feet, with shoulders to match. He was also an active-duty soldier home on leave, with the muscles to prove it. He looked almost indecently sexy in the black sweater and jeans he wore.

She so wasn't going *there,* and jerked her gaze up to his face. "So…?"

"I have a story to tell you."

"Is it about Kennon?"

"Yeah."

"Am I going to want to hear it?"

"I don't know. I hope it will help, but…" He shrugged, looking oddly helpless. "He made me promise to tell you."

She sighed. "He always did think he knew

best about everything."

Gage gave her a crooked smile. "Does that mean you'll listen?"

"I don't want to." A sob squeaked its way past her throat.

"Why?"

"Because then I'll have to admit he's gone. And if this story is about how he died or *why* he died, I might have to give up being angry. I might have to live with the gaping black hole in my life most people call family."

Gage watched her for a moment before asking, "You're afraid?"

She gave him a thin smile that did nothing to conceal the depth of her sorrow. "I'm terrified. He wasn't just my brother; he was my twin. My earliest memory is of laughing with him while we chased a bug across the floor. He was always there for me. *Always.* But I wasn't with him when he needed me."

"I'm sorry," Gage whispered. He took her hand in his. "I really am. I wish I could go back and fix it so he didn't die, but I can't."

That simple gesture of support tore away a small piece of the dam inside her. Grief flowed out the breach, but as with all constructed things, once ruptured, the dam quickly disintegrated, releasing a year's worth of misery all at once.

The pain struck her so hard it was difficult to breathe through the sobs. Her whole body shook. She was blinded by tears and deafened by her own anguish.

Warm hands drew her forward and she encountered a hot wall of muscle covered by a soft sweater. Gage.

His arms wrapped around her, and she buried her head against his chest and cried.

ꕥ

There was a limit to the amount of tears a person could shed.

Kenzie wasn't sure how long she'd cried on Gage's shoulder, but her tea was cold when she finally pulled away to wipe the salty tracks off her face with a few tissues.

"Feel better?" Gage asked in a husky voice that told her he, too, had let himself grieve.

"I feel like someone stuffed this entire box of tissues up my nose."

He chuckled.

"And I have a monster headache." She winced at the damage she'd done to his sweater. "Good grief, you look like someone chucked a bucket of water on you or something."

He pulled the sweater away from his skin and examined it. "I didn't want to say anything, but it's a bit wet."

"Here, take it off. I'll wash it for you."

He looked at her with one eyebrow raised.

"I'll find you something else to wear."

"As long as it doesn't have flowers on it." He stood and pulled off the sweater, handing it to her.

She held out her hand to take it, but her gaze was stuck on the impressive musculature he'd revealed.

Gage was beautifully proportioned. Not outrageously bulked up like a bodybuilder, but nicely defined. *Very* nicely defined.

If the triage nurse had known what he looked like sans shirt, she'd have fought dirty for him.

He cleared his throat and Kenzie realized she'd been staring for far too long. "Sorry. Just wasn't expecting…um, so many…" She gave up trying to finish the sentence and offered him a weak smile. "Sorry."

"I'm not complaining."

That comment jerked her gaze back to his. He was watching her with a strange sort of smile that looked affectionate and…hungry.

No. *No.* He wasn't interested in her. He never had been before. Not when she modeled a bikini accidently on purpose, not even as a mercy date when she confessed she didn't have a date for her convocation. She was imagining things. Strange, crazy things.

She flashed him a smile, pulled the sweater to her chest, and rushed away to the closet where her washer and drier were housed.

Not running away.

Not running away.

Damn straight she was running away. If she was smart she'd keep on going, right out of the apartment and into a whole new zip code.

Gage Remington was dangerous in more ways than she could count. So dangerous, in fact, that she couldn't remember how to operate her own washing machine. Eventually she figured it out and started the sweater on a short wash cycle.

Something told her it was never going to be short enough.

She abandoned the washer for her bedroom closet in hopes of finding something large enough for Gage to wear. If she didn't find something to cover up all that male hotness she might succumb to the temptation to touch all those muscles. He didn't look inclined to stop her.

Okay, so nothing with flowers on it. She went through a pile of sweatshirts, but they were all too small. Finally, she found an old T-shirt of Kennon's that he'd left behind on a visit a couple of years before. She'd forgotten about it and finding it was a punch to the gut all over again.

But it was the only thing that would fit.

She took it out to the living room where Gage stood waiting. She stopped several feet away and held out the shirt as far as she could. He bit his bottom lip like he was having trouble stifling laughter as he took it from her.

"It was Kennon's. I found it in the back of my closet."

And just like that, the mood shifted again, into something somber and sad.

"Thanks." His voice was subdued, almost defeated.

She nodded. "I'm going to make another cup of tea. More coffee?"

"No thanks, but something hot would be good. What kind of tea are you drinking?"

"It's a green tea with some mint. Want to try it?"

"Sure."

The kettle came to a boil and she added water to her teapot. She took the pot and two mugs out to the living room and set them on the coffee table.

Gage had settled on the couch again, but seemed to take up more room than before. She poured the tea and waited for all of two seconds before her feet wanted to be off and doing something other than stay planted on the floor.

She cleared her throat. "So, the story?"

He nodded and took a deep breath. "We were out in the hills on an operation I can't tell you about, in a part of Afghanistan I can't name."

She snorted. "I was never any good at geography anyway."

"We came across a family on an old trail. There were at least three generations of them with what looked like everything they owned either on their backs or on a cart pulled by a couple of old horses. The kids got excited when they saw us and ran ahead of their parents to ask us for chocolate. I think it was one of only five words they knew in English."

He stared into space, his facial muscles moving minutely, telling her he was reliving the moment. She knew that his memory got to a rough part when his whole body jerked. "Bullets rained down on us, creating dirt geysers all around. Two of the kids went down first. Then our lieutenant. The family was screaming and trying to hide under their wagon. Our guys were yelling, trying to find cover and figure out where the shots were coming from."

He was breathing heavily and fast, his fists clenching and unclenching on his lap.

Kenzie slid toward him and took his hand in her own.

He stopped talking for a second, swallowed hard, and held on to her with a grip that she feared would never let her go. Did she want him to let her go? No. No way. She held his hands tighter.

"I got shot in my right shoulder."

"I didn't see a scar."

"It entered from above and behind me and carved a brand-new interstate through my right lung. Hurt like a son of a bitch."

"I didn't know. Show me."

"I haven't told many people, just the family."

She waved that off and rotated her hand in a circle. "Turn around."

He twisted around and pulled the shirt up and over his shoulder. There, just above the blade, was a jagged-edged scar. She stared at it, nausea churning her stomach.

It could have easily killed him. She could have lost Kennon and Gage at the same time. She put her hand on it and traced the uneven outline of the wound with the tip of her index finger. "It looks like it was painful," she whispered.

"Yeah. It hurt, but that wasn't the worst part of it at the time." He let the shirt drop and she pulled her hand away as he turned back around. He didn't let her get far, though, grabbing her hands again and holding on.

"I was having trouble breathing—I guess my lung collapsed—and Ken was right there, covering me, returning fire, and trying to find the SOBs shooting at us."

Gage stopped talking.

Kenzie stared at him for a moment before she realized he'd stopped breathing as well. "Gage?"

"Just give me a second. I haven't told anyone this part."

She slid an inch closer. "Okay."

He took in a couple of breaths that seemed

to calm him down. “One of the kids who’d been shot started to cry and move around. Ken, he ran over and grabbed the kid and plopped him down next to me. The rest of the team were trying to get themselves and everyone else out of the line of fire, but the bullets were coming in from multiple directions, so it was a losing battle.

“One of our guys started using a grenade launcher to return fire and that made a difference. I think he got a few by accident more than design. That’s about when Ken got shot. The first one was in the leg. Which mostly pissed him off. He didn’t move from his position covering that kid and me, just kept firing. The second one got him in the chest. The shooter must have been almost perpendicular to Ken because it got in through his armpit.” Gage paused again, his hands tightening, his face pale. “Ken…went down.” On the last word, Gage’s voice broke and he had to take another breath before continuing. “But he fought back up to his knees and threw himself over me and the kid.” Gage’s composure disintegrated. He started to cry and covered his face with one hand.

She put her arms around him. The selfish part of her wanted him to stop. She didn’t want to picture Kennon’s death, didn’t want to imagine his pain. She didn’t want to put Gage through any more anguish than he was already feeling. “You don’t have to finish. I can guess the rest.”

He grabbed her like she was some kind of lifeline, reeled her in, held on tight, and said into her hair, “No, I have to finish. He made me promise.” Gage nuzzled her neck for a few seconds, as if her scent helped to ground him, then continued. “He looked me in the eye and he said,

'Hey, asshole, I think I'm going to make it into heaven before you do.' I told him he was a greedy jerk and he laughed."

Gage stopped talking to rub his face with both hands, almost as if he was trying to rub the memory out of his mind. "Our guys were shooting, shouting, and shitting bricks." A shaky laugh escaped out of Gage's mouth, a despair-filled sound that sent a cold shiver up her back.

"Then Ken said, 'Promise me something. Survive. Go home. Give my sister the bullet in my chest. Tell her she has to hang on to it until her day comes. Whenever she's got that bullet in her hand, she's holding on to me, you got that?' I said yeah and he said, 'Tell her…'" Gage's voice died for a second then continued softly, so very softly. "'How much you love her.'"

Kenzie froze. *What?*

"A few seconds later he was dead."

She pulled back to look at Gage.

His face was blotchy with tears, yet hot with a blush. He couldn't meet her eyes.

"You…" she began, but she couldn't finish, couldn't put it into words. "Really?"

He finally met her gaze, but only for a second. "Yeah."

This big, strong, attractive guy who could have his pick of women loved her?

"No. That can't be true." How could he have hidden it from her for years? "You're lying."

He looked her in the eye again and didn't drop the contact. "Why would I lie about that?"

"Guilt."

He shook his head. "I feel guilt, but not because of my feelings for you. That might have been the reason if you'd been Ken's wife, but you're his sister."

"Oh." She stared and tried to understand, but it didn't make sense. "If that's how you feel why didn't you tell me this before?"

"You're his sister."

She blinked. "Now I'm confused."

"You'd already lost him to the military and I saw how much you missed him. Then to have a boyfriend in the same situation? I couldn't do that to you. He would have killed me for making you hurt that way." He shook his head with finality. "A man doesn't mess with his best friend's sister."

"What, there are rules?"

"Unwritten, unspoken, undeniable rules," he said with a voice harder than stone.

"That's ridiculous."

"Are you saying women don't have rules about poaching another woman's man or dating a friend's ex?"

"We definitely do have rules for that, but I didn't realize men did. I mean, I know about the 'bros before hos' rule—"

"Completely fabricated by Hollywood."

"Whatever. I just didn't know there were more."

"You're avoiding the subject."

"I…he…you." She blew out a frustrated gust of air. "Men."

Gage stared at her with a small smile. "You're blushing."

He wasn't supposed to notice. "I am *not.*"

"A gentleman would let you get away with it."

She waited all of two seconds before asking,

"Are you a gentleman?"

"Nope. I most definitely am not." He tilted her chin up so she had to meet his gaze. "I'm not letting you off the hook."

She tried to pull away, put some distance between them, but he held her with arms that refused to budge.

"No running away, either," he said, brushing a kiss into her hair.

That quick touch was enough to make her shake. She had yet to come to grips with her brother's death and Gage expected her to take his declaration calmly?

"I don't know if I can handle all this." She sniffed, but instead of giving her some space, he shifted on the couch, reclining a little and pulling her so she rested on his torso, her head snuggled under his chin.

"No need to fuss."

"Fuss?" Such an old-fashioned word.

"I should have told you how I felt ages ago. Ken used to yank my chain regularly about it."

"I don't know what to say." She'd always been attracted to Gage, always wished for more between them, but his friendship with her brother made that secret fantasy impossible. That polite barrier between them had darn near killed her. He only told her now because Kennon made him promise. He probably wouldn't have told her at all if he hadn't been forced into it. Would he come to regret their relationship?

"Don't say anything then."

"But—"

"I didn't tell you so you'd feel bad. I told you because I said I would. *You* don't have to do anything."

"So, you just tell me something you've been keeping to yourself for five years, and I'm just supposed to smile and carry on as if you hadn't said anything?"

"If that's what you want to do, yep."

Was that what she wanted to do? She let herself relax, soaking up his body heat, and for the first time in a long time discovered she felt safe. Whole. Sad, but not immersed in the soul-wrecking pain she'd endured for all the long months since she'd been notified of Kennon's death.

"When I found out Kennon was dead," she said to Gage's shirt. "That he died protecting you—because they told me that much—I was angry."

He rubbed her back in reply.

"I blamed you and I piled all my rage and grief on you."

"Yeah, I figured that's what happened."

"That damned bullet was the *last* thing I ever wanted to see, but…"

"But?"

"Kennon was never one for doing things like anyone else. Why should his death be any different? You were right to give it to me." Her voice fractured on the last word.

"I'm sorry it hurt you so much to see it."

"I think I needed to hurt. I got stuck at the angry stage of grief and didn't know how to get myself out of it, then you came along and knocked me out of my rut."

"That's me, a rut knocker outer."

Alarm bells went off in her head. He was trying to be funny. Trying much too hard. "I thought you weren't going to let me off the hook?"

A subtle tension entered the muscles under her. "Oops."

She lifted her head so she could look him in the eyes. "Well?"

He shrugged. "You're not trying to beat me up, or kill me, so I figure you're doing okay."

She examined his face for deceit and found none, but his tense shoulders told her he was nervous about something. He still had his arms around her, but they were oh so carefully placed. Too carefully.

The entire situation her brother had managed to place both her and Gage in suddenly became clear.

"Kennon never told you, did he?"

"Told me what?"

"That rat." The day she'd discovered her brother reading her diary, he'd teased her without mercy. Reading her most private feelings out loud while she chased him around the room, he'd laughed so hard. She'd been sure he was going to give Gage a few hints.

"Excuse me?"

"That sneaky, underhanded *rat.*" She sat up, pulled out of Gage's arms, and stood next to him with her hands on her hips. "He is without a doubt sitting in heaven laughing his ass off at both of us."

Gage stared at her like she'd lost her mind.

She held out her hand to him. "Come with me."

"Where?"

"Just come."

He took her hand and stood. She towed him out of the living room and down the short hallway to her bedroom.

ꕥ

She flipped on the light, let go of Gage's hand, and went to her dresser to rummage through a drawer.

"I'll just wait out here." Gage pointed at the hallway and began to move away.

"Oh no you don't," she said, grabbing him again and pulling him inside. Kenzie pushed him to sit on the end of the bed. "Stay right there. I want to show you something."

He let out a grunt that sounded frustrated and a little mad. "I'd like to show you something too, but I doubt we're talking about the same thing."

She froze, then turned her head to stare at him. Did he just say what she thought he did?

He rubbed his hands against his jeans-clad thighs. "Sorry."

"No you're not."

He glared at her. "This is not a good idea."

"What isn't?"

"You and me. In your bedroom. Together."

"Nervous?"

The look he gave her could have started a forest fire in the middle of a hard rain. "If you knew what I was thinking you'd be nervous too."

"If I know anything at all, it's that I'm safe with you."

A combination of resolve and despair flowed over his face. It finally solidified into determination and he nodded. "You got me there."

She turned her attention back to the drawer, found the item she was looking for, and hauled it out. Her journal.

She opened it and flipped through the pages. "Here we go." She turned the book around and held it out to Gage. "Read this."

"What is it, your diary or something?"

"Sort of. I wrote all kinds of stuff in there. Dreams, poetry, goals. I stopped writing in it when Kennon died." Gage stared at her with a frown on his face. "Come on, read."

He finally looked at the book in his hands. "The date says three years ago."

She stood in front of him with her hands propped on her hips. "Yeah, and?"

"Bossy," he mumbled as he read. He didn't rush, so she knew when he got to the part she wanted him to see when he suddenly straightened out of his slouch. His gaze jerked up to meet hers.

"Keep reading."

He closed the book and set it carefully onto the floor.

"What are you—" Her voice died as he got to his feet, his eyes going from wide to narrow.

"It says you love me."

"I know what it says. I wrote it."

He took a step forward. "Still feel that way?"

She took a step back, her gaze dancing over his body. "Yes, but you need to see the rest of what I wrote." He stood tall, leaning toward her, his hands reached out to take her by the shoulders and halt her retreat.

He grinned, a slow, sensual slide upward of his lips that told her making him read about her feelings for him in her bedroom might not have been the smartest thing to do.

Or maybe it was exactly right.

"I'll read it later. After I kiss you." He brought her closer, then paused for a brief moment.

"You okay with that?" Even as he asked he was gathering her close, one hand behind her back, the other tangled in her hair, cradling her head.

She'd never been this close, never guessed how good he'd smell, how dwarfed she'd feel in his arms. But instead of that being a bad thing, it was good. She could give someone else control. Give him everything she was, and he'd take exquisite care of it. Of her.

His head came down.

He was going to…

His lips grazed her cheek, her ear. He nipped at the lobe and sucked it into his mouth.

Her eyes slid shut at the pleasure his touch set ablaze inside her.

"Okay?" he asked again.

"What?" Her hands slid around his torso and she lifted herself into his body. Why was he talking? They had more important things to do right now. "Yes, yes."

His mouth came down on hers, his tongue swiping across her bottom lip in a tantalizing tease. She chased it, sucking on it, inviting him to taste her. He didn't hesitate, took what she offered and returned the favor with interest.

So good. His kiss was addicting and delicious. His lips never stopped sipping from her, never stopped taking her into another place where time didn't matter. Only the drugging pleasure his kiss fed into her system.

A large, hot hand cupped her breast and she moaned at the sensation. He molded and squeezed her tender flesh, his fingernail flicking across her nipple, and she jerked in reaction, the jolt of pleasure so acute it shocked her.

She wanted more. She wanted them both naked so she could feel his skin against hers. She'd probably die from pleasure overload, but she didn't care.

She'd denied herself the comfort of other people for so long her body would not be denied any longer.

Her hands groped at the shirt she'd loaned him, shoving it up and out of the way so she could run her hands over his chest. His muscles felt even better than they looked—solid and hard, covered by smooth, soft skin.

Her fingers went to the button on his jeans, then the zipper. She couldn't wait to get her hands on…

"Whoa, slow down." Gage might be out of breath, but he was fast enough to catch her hands with his.

"Party pooper."

He chuckled. "We're not on a time limit, are we?"

"No." It had been so long since she'd felt anything but grief that her pleasure-starved body was greedy for every touch, kiss, and caress. He kissed her, then kissed her again. His breathing jagged. "Damn, but I don't want to stop."

*Yes.* "So don't."

He laughed and stopped kissing her to rest his forehead against hers. "You're a hard woman to resist, Kenzie, but we need to talk a bit more before we do anything else. Because I have a feeling the next thing we do will be on that bed right there with us naked."

She was all for that. "Okay."

"Good." He let out a breath. "You love me?"

"Yes. I have for years."

He let her hands go and stroked her face. "I love you too. Have from the first day I met you."

That long? "I had no idea."

"Well, being Ken's sister meant I had to keep it to myself." He rubbed a thumb over her bottom lip and said, "I remember the first time I saw you. You walked into the room, just home from the gym, and you were sweaty, but all I saw was this gorgeous gal, who damn near glowed and made every cell in my body come to attention. You talked about your job and how you felt it was a calling. A call to service, and I thought, *wow, here's my perfect woman.* Ken took one look at my face and he knew. Told me if I ever touched you, he'd cut my hands off."

"He didn't."

"He did. He took it back a couple of years later, but by then I'd already decided not to tell you. Ken found a way to change my mind, though."

Her brother's name doused her in ice water. "Maybe we shouldn't… I mean—"

"Now, darlin', he's been gone for a year. There's no shame in enjoying what we have together. It's what he wanted."

"I still feel guilty."

He held her a little tighter. "Me too."

Kennon had been gone for a year, and today was Christmas. Maybe it was time she started letting go of her anger and grief. "This all seems like a dream. You really love me?"

His voice rumbled inside his chest. "Yep. I've spent some long, lonely nights thinking about what it would be like to kiss you, touch you."

"Don't think. Let's do."

"I don't want this to be a casual thing, Kenzie. I want all of you."

"What does that mean?"

"An exclusive relationship. You and me. I want to find out if you talk in your sleep and what you look like in the morning after a night of making love." He caressed her hair and face, his fingers lingering on her skin. "I want to find out what brings you the greatest pleasure."

"Are you asking me to…marry you?"

"That's on my list, but I was going to wait a few months yet."

Oh, wow. The idea was a wonderful kind of scary, but one she was sure Kennon would have loved. His sister and his best friend together. "Okay, okay. I can deal with that."

"Yeah?"

"Yeah."

He put a hand under her chin and tilted her head up. "Be sure, because once we get started, I'm not sure I can stop."

The hand cradling her face trembled. Was it possible that she brought this fierce, tough man to a place where he felt that strongly? He'd made himself vulnerable to her. Could she do any less for him?

"I'm sure," she said, covering his hand with hers. "I'm absolutely positive."

He groaned and kissed her.

She kissed him back, her hands rising to slide around him and hold on tight. She had no intention of ever letting him go.

He picked her up, startling a squeak out of her, and laughed as he carried her the few feet to the bed. He followed her down, covering her body with his, one knee between her thighs, and she gloried in his weight.

His hands explored her body with a frenzy that inspired her own sort of crazy.

"Clothes off," she panted, tugging at the shirt he wore, tearing at his jeans.

He pulled her scrub shirt up and over her head. It disappeared somewhere south of the bed. Gage's gaze dropped to her breasts and stayed. "Wow."

She glanced down at her bra, a lacy confection that had cost her a pretty penny. "I wore this to cheer myself up."

He grinned. "Well, it works for me."

She laughed. "You're such a guy."

His hands went around her back and he unhooked her bra, then slid it slowly down her arms.

The bra went south too.

His gaze was hot enough to make her perspire, but when he touched her, cupping both breasts, she darn near set off the fire alarm. His touch was a live wire to her system, lighting her up and setting her off on an exploration of her own.

She attacked his jeans. At least, she tried to. His overwhelming interest in her breasts pulled her astray and into a state where pleasure was all she knew.

"God, you're so responsive," he whispered.

Good Lord, she'd been moaning ever since he got her bra off. "And you're a tease."

"Well, I can't have you saying that." He kissed her again as he coaxed her to lift her hips so he could tug her scrub pants off.

He took one look at her panties, groaned,

and rested his head on her belly.

"Gage? What's wrong?" She looked down to find what she expected, the panties to match the bra.

"Not a damn thing," he said, looking at her. "Your underwear just short-circuited my brain."

"So shut it off. You don't need it right now anyway."

"Truer words have never been spoken." He shucked his jeans and underwear, then donned the condom she handed him from her bedside table drawer. He rejoined her on the bed, kissing her as he covered her and took her in his arms.

His strong, muscular lines fit her curves like he'd been made for her and she found herself crying as he joined his body with hers.

"You okay, darlin'?" His voice was a rumble in her ear.

"Yes," she replied, laughing and crying at the same time. "I'm just a little overwhelmed."

He nuzzled her cheek. "We have all the time in the world."

"But I want…" She had to catch her breath. "I want you to…"

He kissed her again. "I know, and I'm yours."

"I'm yours."

Gage made love to her then and for a long time, it was Kenzie who didn't think at all.

Kenzie woke to a rumbling stomach and a man curled around her like a cat. She rolled to look at him and found him watching her with a smile. "Morning."

"Hi." She stroked her hand over his chest. "I

was half-afraid that yesterday was a dream."

"Nope. All real." He pursed his lips. "What was it you wanted me to read in your journal?"

Her face heated, but she didn't drop his gaze. "I wanted you to see the exact moment I fell in love with you. It was only the second time we saw each other, but you'd helped our neighbor, Mrs. Russell, bring in her groceries after she broke her arm. I don't think you knew anyone saw you, but you were so kind and polite, and so damn hot, I just couldn't keep my eyes off you."

He grinned and kissed her quick. "Get up. I have a gift for you." He climbed out of bed like a sleek panther and picked up his jeans. From the pocket, he pulled out a velvet bag and handed it to her.

Kenzie opened the bag and pulled out a charm bracelet with three gem-colored charms on it. One diamond clear and two emerald green. "Our birth months?"

He nodded. "Do you like it? Is it okay?"

"It's lovely." She tilted her head to one side. "But you already gave me the best gift ever."

"I have?"

"You."

"That gift wasn't from me. It was from Ken. He's the one who sent me here."

Joy at the happiness of their future together and sadness from the grief of losing her twin combined to rain tears down her face. "My Secret Santa."

"Mine too," Gage said, turning onto his back and drawing her across his chest. "Mine too."

About…

Julie Rowe's first career as a medical lab technologist in Canada took her to the Northwest Territories and northern Alberta, where she still resides. She loves to include medical details in her romance novels, but admits she'll never be able to write about all her medical experiences because, "No one would believe them!" In addition to writing contemporary and historical medical romance, and fun romantic suspense for Entangled Publishing and Carina Press, Julie has a short story in *The Mammoth Book of ER Romance* (September 2013). Her book *Saving the Rifleman* (book one of the War Girls series) won the novella category of the 2013 Gayle Wilson Award of Excellence. Her writing has also appeared in several magazines such as *Today's Parent, Reader's Digest* (Canada), *Canadian Living,* and *Romantic Times Magazine.*

For more information about Julie, please visit her online at www.julieroweauthor.com, on Twitter @julieroweauthor, or at her Facebook page: www.facebook.com/JulieRoweAuthor.

Interested in reading more medical romance and adventure? Check out Julie's published backlist of books!

Julie's War Girls series is set in German-occupied Belgium during World War One. Discover danger, daring, and passion with three nurses who risk their lives to save the men they call their own.

***Saving the Rifleman*** - John and Maria's story.
***Enticing the Spymaster*** - Michael and Jude's story.
***Aiding the Enemy*** - Herman and Rose's story.

For contemporary stories of adventure and romance set at the top and the bottom of the world, look for ***Icebound*** and ***North of Heartbreak*** at your favorite ebook retailer.

Coming Summer 2014

# Timeless Escapes

## A Collection of Summer Stories

Ruth A. Casie

Lita Harris

Emma Kaye

Nicole S. Patrick

Julie Rowe

CPSIA information can be obtained at www.ICGtesting.com
Printed in the USA
LVOW10s1526040314

376008LV00017B/973/P

9 780991 052011